Tales from the Silver State III

Tales from the Silver State III

Short Fiction from Nevada's Freshest Voices

Noëlle de Beaufort
Karen Bryant • Jay Hill
John Hill • Hyrum Husky
Patricia Kranish • Holly Mack
Carole McKinnis • Ernest Walwyn
Richard J. Warren

Edited by Richard J. Warren

Muddy Pig Press • Las Vegas, Nevada

Photo Credit: © Can Stock Photo Inc./mariait

Cover Credit: John Hill

ISBN-13: 978-0692606766
ISBN-10: 0692606769

Printed in the United States of America

www.muddypigpress.com

Muddy Pig Press • Las Vegas, Nevada

Dedicated to the Memory of
Jay MacLarty

Many a trip continues long after movement in time and space have ceased.
– John Steinbeck

Table of Contents

Editor's Note 1

Morning Coffee at the Dinosaur Ranch: *John Hill* 3

Spare Change: *Holly Mack* 21

Lake Lahonton: *Patricia Kranish* 41

Aleatory Nevada: *Jay Hill* 55

Who Sits at the Left Hand of God?: *C. McKinnis* 69

Oracle in a Red Coat: *Karen Bryant* 81

Snakes: *Hyrum Husky, Jr.* 101

The Flight of the Eagle Feather: *N. de Beaufort* 111

Walking the Bristlecone Trail: *Ernest Walwyn* 133

Granddaddy's Gun: *Richard J. Warren* 145

Meet the Authors 157

The Las Vegas Writers Group 169

Editor's Note

The first edition of Tales from the Silver State was released in early 2014. The collection was assembled as a way to honor the legacy of Jay MacLarty, a Simon & Shuster author and founder of the Las Vegas Writers Group. Jay envisioned the group as a place where writers could come together to learn from one another and support each other as they practiced their craft. Many writers have passed through this group on their way to finding success as authors. Several of them were invited to contribute to that inaugural volume as a way to pay tribute to Jay.

The success of that first edition made the decision to publish a sequel an easy one. This year marks the third volume of the anthology. The members of the LVWG, now numbering more than 400, were invited to submit tales for this edition of *Tales from the Silver State*. The many submissions were judged anonymously by a panel of readers and the best stories were chosen for publication. Those are the tales you will read here.

Assembling an anthology would not be possible without the help and support of others. Acknowledgement and thanks to the contributing authors: Noëlle de Beaufort, Karen Bryant, Jay Hill, John Hill, Hyrum Husky, Patricia Kranish, Holly Mack, Carole McKinnis, Ernest Walwyn, and Richard J. Warren.

Special thanks to the creative writing faculty and students at the University of Nevada, Las Vegas for their assistance with this project. As always, thanks to the "piglets" on staff at the Muddy Pig Press for making this anthology possible.

Morning Coffee at the Dinosaur Ranch

By John Hill

Luke Harding, in his favorite red plaid shirt, faded jeans, and cowboy boots made from pterodactyl wings, stepped out that morning on the front porch of his old ranch house, as he did every morning. He sat down in his father's old wooden rocking chair, now his, holding a cup of coffee. He tried ignoring the arthritis in his right knee, failed. Being 62 years old for Luke was some strength still in his unbent six foot body, pewter gray hair but lots of it, an unshaven, craggy but handsome face, eyes good, hearing and knee starting to go.

Should have gotten my jacket, he thought, rocking slowly, sipping coffee, looking out over the vast green and blue vista. He always enjoyed this majestic view, his ranch, the green acreage, the low white wooden fences, for the cattle and horses, larger gray metal fences for the dinosaurs, sloping down slowly. Then, a brief valley, then a gently sloping up to the distant blue Nevada mountains, white at the tops. Pale yellow morning sunlight was slowly bullying away the purple night shadows. The last wisps of morning ground fog lent a mystical quality to the imaginative, annoying temporary gray to the realistic. Luke loved it all, always had. He loved the land, the animals.

This was Luke's favorite time of day, same porch, same view, for almost sixty years. As a boy, he loved joining his father and grandfather having their morning coffee out here, (he got hot chocolate), enjoying the view (his grandfather adding a little whiskey to his coffee, winking at little Luke), the two men talking ranching. Time, and his older brother, Death, had stopped by, done their usual damage; his grandfather and father both long gone now. And Death, maybe it was a case of, while you're up? He took Luke's wife too.

Luke glanced over at the empty wooden chairs, wishing his handsome, on-the-bounce son, Jack, 24, was sitting there, with him, as he should be. Instead, Jack was still in town after another night of playing that fucking blackjack. Luke wanted his son, by now, to be happily married, kids too, with a love for the ranch he'd own one day. But Jack's passion, bizarrely, was green felt, not green grass. How could that be?

How in the hell could he not be here for this?

Luke looked at the distant purple brontosauruses he owned, their slowing moving heads in the morning sunlight; what's not to love? Instead of appreciating, then planning, a day of work on the ranch, father and son now only argued about gambling debts. Every hand dealt to Jack broke Luke's heart just a little more. He didn't know how to get his son back. Jack. God help me. Never saw this one coming. Three years ago, he loved...all this, the ranch, the lifestyle. Then he turned 21. And the casinos legally sucked him in, but he went willingly...Jack must need the energy of a casino, not the slow motion nature of daily ranching...or am I making excuses for him?

Luke sighed, sipped his coffee. It was May, still cold in the mornings. He could see the thick grayish breath from one of the stegs in the fenced-in small herd of light green-skinned stegosauruses over to the right, one hundred yard away. The twenty stegs were his main meat crop; steg steaks tasted the best. And stegs were the easiest to raise and keep, as a meat crop, by their pleasant temperament, easy as raising cattle.

He wanted more coffee, and his jacket, but both were way inside. With his knee? A goodly distance. He hope his friend and neighbor, Cal, from the next ranch over, would stop by today. Cal was a rock.

The (less tasty) huge purple and light blue

brontosauruses, seven of them, towered over their twenty-foot fences; they were a cheaper meat, but you got tons of it from just one. The wind shifted. Luke could smell the closer stegosaurus herd now, an odor he had gotten used to as a boy. Luke sipped his coffee.

Luke's grandfather back in the 1920's had built this old Nevada ranch house higher up on the hill, for this view. There were still wild dinos in those days, he had said, telling his stories, the small herds of triceratops being the worst problem then, their massive heads and spiked horns. Even just half a century ago, they roamed wild, tearing up fences, the barn, tool shed, fast as 12-year-old Luke, his grandfather and his father could build or repair them. But the raw natural wildlife was a little tamer now, in 2015, and today's technology, sensors, ranch radar, tracking dinos, domesticated, even a few wild ones, but the wild West? Not so wild anymore. A loss.

Luke squinted, smiled, treated this morning to the distant tiny lines in the sky, catching the thermals near the mountains. He liked seeing the wild pterodactyls, their 30-foot wingspans, free, scorning modern civilization. On rare occasions, they would swoop down with a mighty screech and carry off a cow or a sheep, so a thirty-ought-six rifle was in every pick-up truck, on every chore on the ranch.

Then Luke saw the familiar old rusty-red, monster pickup truck, giant wheels, cab sitting up high, drive into view, and up the winding road, towards the ranch house. Luke got up, wincing when his right knee got some of his weight, went in, and came back with his jacket on, a refill on his coffee, and a big, oversized ten-inch-high mug for his old friend. Cal had parked his big pick-up truck and was walking up the hand-built brick walkway to the porch, as Luke set Cal's big cup of coffee down on the huge wooden chair, Cal's special big chair, ten feet from his. Luke sat down again.

"I see you, favorin' that knee," Cal said, in his gravelly deep voice.

"You can't hardly see the house, your eyesight now," Luke grumbled back, making himself stop rubbing his knee. Cal came up the old wooden stairs, which creaked, protesting his immense weight. But the stairs were used to Cal. Luke was too. Talk about time. Cal and Luke had been friends since, as Cal once put it, Noah heard thunder.

Cal was a raptor, a bi-ped, gnarly claw-like hands, high hipbones and legs. He wore raptor clothes, these for ranching, a shirt, jeans, huge boots, light jacket. Cal was in his 60's too, and he and Luke had played together as boys, lifelong friends. Cal's 440 pounds made the old wooden porch creak loudly as he came up the stairs, and then sat in his oversized rocking chair, picking up his big coffee cup, nodding his thanks. Cal sighed, also feeling his age this morning.

"Jack still enjoying last night?" Cal asked, in his raspy raptor voice, gesturing to Jack's conspicuously empty wooden chair. Luke nodded, sourly. "Hey, did you watch that PBS documentary last night?" Cal said, smiling, quickly changing the subject.

"Forgot about it," Luke said. "Any good?"

"Not really," Cal said. "Covered the usual, why is it raptors evolved with heightened intelligence, a voice box, and an opposable claw-thumb, and all the rest stayed just big dumb lizards, that stuff, about fifth-grade level. No new insights."

"They didn't all evolve with higher intelligence," Luke said. "I've seen you try to work the last latch on your steg corral lock."

"It's just broken, you know that, Jeez," Cal said shaking his two-foot-long, reptilian head to himself.

"What's the latest theory on why you're drinking my coffee instead of being down there in one of those pens?"

"You mean why we finally let you humans out of your cages?"

"You always think our centuries of slavery is somehow funny," Luke grumbled. Cal ignored his lack of humor this morning, and went on. "We've always been bi-peds, worked together in hunting packs, like humans, that was the reason our language skills developed, same for thumbs," Cal said. "More coffee where this came from?" Luke gestured inside, so Cal got up, and talked louder as he went in for the coffee pot, came back, sat down. They each stretched their legs out a little, enjoying the calm early hours and sweet sunlight crawling over the ranch and the gorgeous mountain view. The rest of the day, very soon, would be work.

Then a big green pick-up pulled up to the farm, one Hispanic driving, four Hispanic workmen in back, Luke's ranch hands. The pick-up parked, the four men in back jumped out, putting on work gloves, finished chatting in Spanish. One each headed for the horse corral, cattle fences, the steg pen and the brontosaurus's tall metal fencing. The driver, Hector, 57, walked up towards the porch.

"Good morning, Mr. Luke," he said. "Mr. Cal." Slight accent.

"Careful of your boss today, Hector," Cal said. "He's a grouchy bear."

"Don't pay any mind to the porch lizard, Hector," Luke said. "He wouldn't know a good day's work if he ever did one."

Hector asked Luke about some ranch chores, Luke gave him some priorities, and Hector, the foreman, walked back, joined his men.

"You feel like talkin' this morning, about Jack," Cal said, in a different tone, "I can hear just fine, not like you."

Luke sighed, said, "Thanks, but..." Waved it away. They sipped their coffee. But then Cal and Luke were both distracted, by the unusual sight of half a dozen vehicles coming up the road, towards Luke's ranch house. A police car in front, then a huge truck, the one's designed for dino-transport, two more cars, and a pick-up.

"What the hell we got here?" Cal said, out loud, more to himself.

"That's Jack's yellow pick-up, bringing up the rear," Luke said, quietly getting to his feet. "Well, this looks like Jack's way of coming home now...dear Lord, what fresh cluster fuck is this?"

"Looks like he's bringing some big animal home with him," Cal said, standing up too, staring. "That's a specially reinforced dino-truck."

"And of course, leading Cal's arrival," Luke said, "is a cop. Jesus..."

Luke sighed, and started walking down the stairs, to

meet Jack's latest problem. His morning had been nice until now. Until his son. Goddamned Nevada casinos...

"Good morning," said the young patrol cop, in uniform, as he got out of the squad car. "Are you Luke Harding, father of Jack Harding?"

"Yes."

"Mr. Harding, I'm Officer Joe McGentry, from the Colby, Nevada, Police Department. I'm the local liaison cop with the raptor casino, five miles from town. I'm only here in an advisory or pre-emptive protective capacity. This is a civil matter. I'll let your son and the others explain." And with that, Officer McGentry tipped his hat and got back in his car, leaving Luke to turn and look at Cal, who was now beside him. Cal shrugged. Whatever this was, it wasn't good.

The two in business suits, one human, one raptor, emerged from one car, then four workmen in rough, farm clothes. Bringing up the rear was Jack Harding, young, handsome, tired, in a sport jacket, looking glum.

The two businessmen were walking up towards Luke, smiling, as one was getting paperwork out of a briefcase, but Jack caught up with them, leaned in, talked quietly, they stopped, waiting, thirty feet back, as Jack hurried up to his father and Cal.

"Hey, Dad," Jack said, nervously, walking up to them.

"Uncle Cal."But Luke and Cal just waited, looking at him. Jack hadn't shaved, hair a little mussed, he clearly hadn't slept all night.

"You, uh, probably want to know what's going on, huh?" Jack said.

"No, no," Cal said. "This is the Macy's Thanksgiving Day Parade, and the big ol' Snoopy float will be along soon. I love that float."

"Yeah, uh..." Jack said, then finally looked Luke in the eye. "So Dad, I screwed up last night. Lost some serious money playing blackjack, then borrowed more to try to win it back, you know."

"No, son, I don't know," Luke said. "I really don't know about that."

"Well, the thing is, I lost that money too, so the casino executives, they decided to take a promissory note from me, and I kept gambling." Jack gulped, since looking at his father's face for any sympathy was like looking for it on the faces at Mt. Rushmore. "Well, I lost that money, and we made a deal. They're here to, you know, take one of the stegs, for what I owe. You know...now."

"Take one of the stegs?" Luke repeated, stunned. Cal just rolled his eyes, then shook his large head to himself. "Take one of the stegs?"

"Well, you know, Dad," Jack said, looking down, "ever since you gave me half the ranch, when I turned 21, well, this steg they'll take can just be one of mine, okay?"

There was only the sound of the distant moaning-growls from the steg pen, the cattle lowing in their pens. Everyone waited.

"Market value of a single steg is at bout $18,000-$19,000 now?" Cal said. "That sound right to you, Luke?"

"Nothing about this sounds right," Luke said, staring hard at Jack.

Jack gestured to the men behind him. "See, we made a deal, that instead of me not having the cash, and those, uh, problems, they'd agree to accept one of my stegs instead, first thing this morning."

Luke was too stunned to even speak. Cal said nothing.

They choose the biggest stegosaurus, naturally, herded him into the truck, legal paperwork was signed. Then the entire circus drove away, Hector telling the ranch hands to get back to work, leaving Jack holding receipts, paperwork, standing there. He finally looked up at the porch, where Luke and Cal were now sitting, watching.

Cal spoke quietly to Luke, "I'd leave but I'm afraid you'll kill him."

"Well, he's killing me," Luke said, quietly.

"I know."

But Cal left, after he paused beside Jack, and leaned in close, briefly, saying, quietly, "You're cutting him deep. You can grow up anytime, Jack." Then Cal had gotten in his big truck, drove away, leaving the two men there, and the ranch, minus one steg.

Luke gestured for Jack to come up, sit in his usual porch chair, so Jack did, apologizing his way up the stairs. Luke held up a hand, stop. Jack sat down, awkwardly holding the receipt and paperwork, not knowing what to do with them. Luke turned to him.

"Two months ago, you gambled away three cattle," the father said. "Three of our cattle, since you had gone through your own cash, and still kept playing blackjack. And we had us quite a talk about you and gambling, right?"

"Yes, sir," Jack said, "and I'm sure sorry about last night --"

Luke held up his hand, waiting for Jack to be quiet. Jack shut up. Luke rubbed his face with his hands, leaned forward, signed, then looked over at his son. "I should really think on this, even give you a chance to tell your side of things, but the hell with that. Here's the deal, from this moment on." He paused, got up, wincing because of his right knee. "Just sit here, don't talk, don't go away." Luke went into his living room, trying to control his anger. The old photographs framed on the wall, of his father, his grandfather, the early days of the ranch, always made him feel good. Now he saw their eyes on him. Staring. Glaring. From beyond their graves, up on the hill, they were counting on him. Luke looked around the old ranch living room, the big stone fireplace, the sofas made of softened steg skin, sighed, went back out on the porch, knowing he should think this out more, but fuck that.

"I am way beyond enraged," Luke said, sitting back down. "If I thought it would do any good, I'd drag you off this porch and beat the living crap out of you. But I don't think that would help you, or me. Plus, you're a grown man. You're 24, not 15, so you are free to do what you want, technically. And take the consequences. But your immature choices, or your addiction, is a whirlpool that could eventually drag down our lives now and almost a hundred years of a family ranch. The potential for that exists today. You could ruin my life, my father's past, your future, you're on the way to wrecking it all, past, present, future. You see, my dream is that someday you'll be the old guy on this porch, and you'll have a grandchild running the place. I'm going to fight for that dream. Now. In this way."

Luke paused. Jack just gulped and had the sense to just listen.

Luke watched the distant brontosaurus pen, with its 20 feet high, steel-reinforced fence, and the two bronts leaning over, near each other. That's Happy and I think Sneezy, Luke thought. Look at what a peaceful day they're having, and I'm not.

"Since you are totally out of control and represent a very real threat to the security of this ranch, you and I are going to my lawyer's office tomorrow. You, Jack, will sell me back your half ownership of this ranch, which I gave you on your 21st birthday, back to me for one dollar. That way, you are no longer an owner of any of the livestock or land or anything else on this ranch. You cannot legally lose any of it at a blackjack table. I'll send a letter to all casinos within five hundred miles with a copy of that document so they all know not to advance you any markers based on your co-ownership of a small dinosaur ranch."

Jack was staring, at all this, mouth open, beyond stunned.

Luke went on to explain Jack was now on a very limited salary, and his spending would be monitored, all for the next year. Then Luke got up, made himself breakfast of eggs and a steg steak, then started his day's work on the ranch. Jack went to bed, slept.

The next afternoon at 4 p.m., Luke and Jack and Cal were all sitting in Luke's lawyer's office, signing quickly-prepared legal papers. When they left, Jack had signed away all ownership, Cal signing as a witness. Luke told the lawyer he'd be back in next week, to sign a new will, which put Luke's ranch and estate into a trust, to be managed by Cal, who would decide when or if Jack ever inherited anything. Cal didn't join them for their next stop, at the bank, where Luke set up completely different checking, savings, and business accounts. Luke then drove he and Jack home, telling Jack to call the bio-waste recycling company, to send their trucks out today.

Three weeks passed, three weeks of Jack's moody, silent new way of life, hard work, having to defend every penny he would get from his father, three weeks of an uncomfortable tension between father and son. But, while sullen, Jack seemed to accept these new rules.

Then one day, about 3 p.m., when Jack had been sent into town on an errand, he drove back, pick-up weaving, due to his drunken state, and all hell broke loose. Everything happened fast. Hector and two of the ranch hands almost had to jump out of Jack's way, in his truck. He was honking the horn, screaming. "I lost $700 just now!" Jack yelled to no one, "so the fuck what? I'm a grown man, this is my ranch too!"

Luke had been inside, going over the books, when he heard the honking, then Hector's man pounding on the door. Luke ran to look outside, instantly knew Jack had snapped. He hit speed dial on his cell phone as he ran down the stairs, phoning Cal, saying "Get over here fast, please!" and ran towards Jack's truck.

But Jack had already opened the driver's door, and had fallen out of it, onto the ground. His hair was mussed, shirttail out, holding a bottle of bourbon with one hand, screaming, as he got up and staggered to the bront gate, "THIS IS MINE TOO, YOU CAN'T TAKE IT AWAY FROM ME! I CAN DO WHAT I WANT ON THIS RANCH!" And as Luke was running from the house towards Jack, he knew he wouldn't get there in time. Jack staggered towards the bront gate lock, angrily waving Hector and the confused ranch hands away. Yelling how he could do what he wanted, Jack punched in the gate code, and the huge twenty-foot high metal gates started to swing open, freeing the seven brontosauruses. Both Luke and Hector were yelling, "NO! NO!" but it was too late. The metal steel gates were slowly, steadily opening, and the nearest bront, Doc, was curious and walking towards the new opening, a very leisurely escape...

The huge lumbering beast never even saw Hector as it knocked him down and one large front foot buried Hector in the soft, moist ranch soil, as it lumbered on out -- Hector's blood on his foot as it meandered out into temporary freedom--

In the horrible afternoon that followed, the bront herded back into its pen, Sheriff Bill Dodge arrived. He privately told Luke he could write this up as another dinosaur ranching accident, an aspect of the business which everyone knew could happen, and not put it down as Jack's fault. He quietly said he'd do whatever his old friend, Luke, wanted. Cal had stood nearby, hearing this choice, as did Jack, while Hector's remains were carefully, gently, scooped up with a shovel, placed in a body bag, then put in the medical examiner's car. Luke had looked over at his son, then Hector's body, then, without emotion, told the sheriff exactly what had happened, and to write it up that way, knowing it would send Jack to jail. A confused Jack was put in handcuffs, taken away.

Eight months later, the day after the trial -- Cal made sure Jack got the best lawyer possible -- when Jack was sentenced to four years for manslaughter in Nevada State Prison -- Cal drove over that morning to have his morning coffee with Luke. For them to look out over the beautiful ranch and distant mountains would be a good thing today, Cal thought. Luke might even spot the distant pterodactyls flying over the mountains. Maybe the sight of them would make the still stoic Luke smile, even though he had just sacrificed four years of his son's life to try to save both Jack and the ranch. A huge sacrifice. Luke was gambling on Jack's prison time to save the ranch and save his son. And Jack thought he was a gambler, Cal mused.

Cal pulled up in his big monster truck, parked, seeing Luke was up on his porch, already having his morning coffee. But as Cal got out and started walking up to join him, he stopped. Cal saw something he had never seen happen with his friend, not in fifty years. Luke was sitting in his usual chair, his beloved ranch, now safe from his son, spread out before him, and Luke had his head down and was crying so hard his body was shaking, his coffee spilling.

Cal didn't know whether to go up and try to comfort his friend, or leave him alone for now and just drive away. In the distance, unnoticed, behind him, a thousand feet in the air, pterodactyls caught the thermals and soared, wild and free.

The End

Spare Change

By Holly Mack

The first time Larina heard the voice, she stopped at the light and stared toward the Stratosphere Tower, her eyes fixed on the carnival rides on the top. The intermittent screams of the bungie jumpers echoed across the lanes of traffic with all the terror and excitement of a second-rate horror flick.

"The world will end."

'Shut the fuck up,' she thought. 'It will not.' As the newest psychic on swing shift at Crystal Aura, she made every effort to stand out from the crowd of seers and witches. She dressed in a suit, wearing a recent version of the year's fashion. The last thing she needed on her drive to work was a disembodied voice giving a countdown to the apocalypse.

"The world ends here."

"Yeah, I know," she muttered, changing the stream on her I-pod, hoping different music would bring a different message. "You already said that." Surely Pandora had something to drown out the voice. Classical music should do the trick. Violins and flutes appealed to her at the moment, so she hit the screen, and Beethoven's Ninth roared through the speakers. The ominous chords crashed, trying to shake her from the driver's seat. When the light changed, she tightened her grip on the steering wheel and pressed the gas as the car eased off the strip and onto Sahara.

Ten minutes later she pulled into her parking space behind the strip mall, her nerves jangled and her head pounding. She grabbed her purse and started for the door.

A dark form materialized out of the asphalt, an apparition of woe and defeat. "Spare change?"

Larina felt in her pocket and tossed out some coins, hoping to avoid more interaction.

"Hey! Yer a psychic. Ain't cha? I seen ya going in there." He motioned toward the Crystal Aura's backdoor.

"Yes, I am," she said, not breaking stride.

"What cha see for me? My future, I mean."

Larina turned, "Look," she started, ready to give her canned explanation on how she didn't work for free, and her time was valuable, blah blah. She stopped, stunned by his appearance. Death looked out of the man's face. A skull smiled, using the man's own broken and stained teeth.

She sighed, "You need to contact your family," she said. "Get in touch with your children." She knew he wouldn't, but for their sake she tried.

The man scowled and hacked a gob of thick phlegm onto the ground between them. "Mind yer own bidness."

She turned away. So much for charity work.

The receptionist greeted her with a bored face as he pushed the log toward her. "Hi, Loraine."

"La-reen-ah," she corrected for the hundredth time. Her mouth was on automatic, but her mind was on the end of the world.

He ignored her side of the conversation. "Tarmack the Infallible is off tonight. You'll have to fill in." He ran his finger down a column on the page and stopped at an entry. "His first client will be here in about . . ., he glanced at the clock, the face of which protruded out of a cherub's behind, "five minutes. I'll send him over."

Larina nodded and walked to the back of the shop, not stopping to make her usual cup of tea. She pulled aside the drape which covered the entrance of her cubicle, and secured it with a chain. Her nose wrinkled as she caught a whiff of patchouli-infused incense and the reek of marijuana. Couldn't Farin smoke that crap at home? Why did she have to bring it to work forcing the rest of them to suffer the skunk fumes?

Larina locked her purse in a cabinet next to her chair and sprayed her glass-topped desk with cleaner, rubbing the streaks away in a counter-clock-wise motion. "I am not staying here," she intoned, filling the ritual with emotion. She felt she would never leave this job. She would come in day after day, give reading after reading and eventually, one day, she would die, and someone else would take over. But only, she reminded herself, if the voice was wrong and the world didn't end.

A soft cough at her doorway interrupted her thoughts, and she looked up at her customer, a professional smile glued to her lips. "Please come in," she gestured to the chair across from her.

The man wore an outdated version of Yuppie casual, but the balding head and overly careful pony tail ruined his prosperous look. He looked at her set-up, disappointment written large across his face. "You the reader?"

At his tone, she felt her smile slip, but ducked her head to open the small wooden box on her desk. "Tarot?" she offered.

The man pulled back the chair and lowered into it as if afraid it would stick to him. "Tarmack usually has me pick items from a bowl."

"Yes, he's a . . . ." What the exactly was he? "An

innovator. Very progressive. The shop is lucky to have him."
She stopped short of telling the guy he should come back
when Tarmack was in. What was she thinking? She needed his
money. "What's your name?"

"Simon, Simon Bonneville. I'm in real estate."

She picked up the cards and shuffled. "So Simon,
when were you born?"

"Seventy-two. I'm the youngest. I have four older
sisters, but finally, I came." He smiled with modest pride.

No need to actually read his cards. They would show
his inability to interact with women, and he would wonder
why all his relationships ended badly, and why everyone
seemed to turn against him in the end. No doubt Tarmack the
Infallible called in to avoid him.

She flipped over the first card, the ace of pentacles. Of
course, she thought, money. The seven of pentacles crossed
that one. Oh joy, he came from a religious family. Probably
went to the kind of church where he would confess the sin of
going to a psychic, get forgiveness and come back the very
next week. "I see that you have recently made a large
investment, and that you are a man of devotion and
dedication, blah, blah."

Half an hour later, he was gone and she was twenty
dollars richer. More lost souls came out of the night to sit

across from her. At the end of her shift, she walked into the morning, watching as the fingers of the sun slowly tore away the night, turning the brilliant neon darkness into the pastels of dawn.

"Today the world ends."

She woke to the voice's dire pronouncement. A glance at the clock beside her bed showed old fashioned hands, three p.m. on the dot. The alarm beeped as she peered with near-sighted intensity at the face. A quick smack shut it down. She groaned and climbed out of bed half walking half stumbling into the shower. Knowing she would have a full Friday night's worth of waiting tables, gave her hope for her finances. Her feet ached. They hated her and her insistence on working a job with mileage involved. Good thing tipsy guests left generous tips. The tokes were great at the start of the weekend. Her toes could just toughen up.

She arranged her hair in a tight braid, and buttoned her shirt all the way before tying a bright red bow around the collar. She stared into the mirror wondering how she had fallen so far off track. Her education should mean a management track, but the voices in her head meant odd jobs and lots of them. Dismissing her lost future with a shrug, she slung her purse over her shoulder and started out to work.

The sun glared in full-on flare mode as the walk to her

car seared her nose hairs. If she moved too slowly, her feet sank into the heat-softened asphalt. One incautious step and the sole of her shoe collected a tail of chewing gum. The tenacious substance clung to her foot stringing out from her doorstep all the way to her car. She scraped her sole on the frame before she slid behind the wheel. *Great*, she thought, *another chore to add to her list.* Wash the car and scrape the bubble gum off the paint. As she exited the lot, her mind traveled to a world where considerate neighbors disposed of their sputum-infused treats in a hygienic manner.

With a minimum of traffic hassle, she wheeled up to the employees' lot. Sliding her badge through the reader to lift the bar of the gate, she wondered, not for the first time, why her employers thought they needed a lock on the absolute worst parking on the property.

"Hey, Larina." Miguel Eastwind hailed her with a wave. He worked as a busboy at night, but in the day he attended UNLV as a food and beverage student.

A sweet guy, she thought, deciding not to tell him that this week he would be better blowing off work and trying to get lucky. Being the end of the world and all. "Hi, Miguel. You ready for the Football Friday fun fest?"

He mimed tucking a ball under one arm and strong-arming a blocker out of his way. "Sure am," he laughed. "I'm working your section."

Larina felt her heart warm with a small glow. Working with Miguel felt like dancing with a great partner. They both understood the choreography of the job as well as the positions of the tables. Ten years younger than her twenty-nine, he always came to work cheerful and eager to start.

Linking arms and matching steps, they sang the song from the *Wizard of Oz*. Their mood continued happy and light as the afternoon proceeded with a smoothness the previous night lacked. Larina got all the orders right, regardless of what the customers actually said, and unlike other busboys, Miguel never second-guessed her checks at the counter.

Diners came in hungry and crabby. They left sated and thrilled with her lucky guesses and perfect service. Midnight arrived and with it the closing of her section. Now only the bartenders and a single short-order cook would remain.

"Wanna go for a beer?" Miguel pulled off his uniform jacket and shook it before folding it into a tidy square bundle.

Was he asking her out? No, that couldn't be. The decade between their birthdates precluded any romance. She pulled up her schedule on her phone. Oh joy, she thought, the resurrection shift at Crystal Aura. Quitting time meant nine in the morning, but starting time was three a.m. She had two options. Hang out and nap in her car until three rolled around, or grab a cold one with Miguel before clocking in to her psychic gig. No contest. End of the world or not, her social skills needed to be dusted off. "Where to?"

"Fireflies' is right down the street." He flashed his heart-breaking smile. "We could grab something to eat."

She hesitated. The last time she had eaten there, all hell had broken loose and ruined an otherwise lovely evening. The details of the conflagration came to her in nightmares, but for the most part she tried to forget the demonic war fought out of her favorite tapas restaurant. Miguel's innocent face started to read disappointment. Why ruin his evening? "Sure, that sounds great." Crap, she thought. No wonder the voice kept yacking on and on about the end of the world.

Miguel opened her car door for her and she scooted out to stand on the pavement. A block east of the strip Fireflies fed and watered herds of tourists. With luck they could have a short wait and a seat at the bar. The hostess bared shiny white teeth in Miguel's direction, but her eyes narrowed at the sight of Larina.

"I can seat you immediately, if you don't mind sitting at the bar." She started walking towards the back, not waiting to see if they objected. They followed her almost running. Whatever luck they had in scoring a seat with promptness could be lost if they dawdled.

The bartender slapped two coasters down in front of their empty stools. "What can I make for you?"

"Sangria," Larina said in chorus with Miguel. She wondered if she truly wanted sangria, or if her mind tuned itself to his.

The bartender, whose name tag said Louis, set the pitcher down and slid two goblets toward them, red wine and fruit shimmering in the flickering light of the fake candles.

As soon as the liquid hit her tongue, she groaned with pleasure. Crisp, sweet with just a hint of whiskey to kick her blues away. "Thanks," she gasped as she came up for air. "I needed that."

"How about some tapas?" Miguel plucked the menu card from behind the napkins and laid it on the bar between them.

Larina ran her eyes from the top of the hot plate list all the way to the coldest of chilled gazpacho. "I could go for some bacon wrapped dates."

"Something sweet wrapped in meat." He leaned toward her with a comic leer, his eyebrows wiggling up and down.

She laughed. "Sounds disgusting when you say it like that."

"We are getting an order of those," he announced. "And we're having an order of ahi. Cause fish is brain food, and my brain is hungry."

"Is that what they teach you kids in school these days?"

"Laugh if you want, old lady, but I am learning the occult art of feeding the masses."

They grinned at each other and spun their chairs to look out over the patrons and beyond them into the street where cars drove bumper to bumper in their love/hate dance of red and green lights. A silver Porsche caught her eye. "Is that one yours?" she asked, knowing he could never afford the creamy perfection of the two door convertible.

"Yes, yes it is." At her startled look he continued. "I stole it fair and square."

She laughed, feeling the alcohol smoothing the edges of her day. "You work as a valet as well? That must kill your love life."

His eyes met hers. How can you say that? I'm sitting here next to a beautiful woman enjoying fine wine. Okay maybe crappy wine, but it's sangria." He lifted his glass in a toast, and gestured toward the young waitress just arriving with their order. "Fabulous food. What more could a man ask?"

"No time," the voice announced.

Couldn't it leave her alone for one night? She dropped her head as she sipped her sangria.

"No time for what?" Miguel asked.

"Sorry, did you say something?"

He pointed to a space somewhere over her right shoulder. "I was talking to him, that creepy guy that follows you around and talks at you all the time."

"You can see him?" Her breath caught in her throat.

"I sure can. Boy is he pissed off."

"He talks about the end of the world," Larina said. "He's quite intense."

Miguel's face twisted in annoyance. "Which world?" he asked. "The one we create for ourselves out of the ashes of yesterday, or the one we put the torch to when we sleep?"

"You could save the world, if you aren't too self-centered."

They turned toward the voice, but Larina couldn't see anything. "How?" they asked.

"A little sacrifice."

Crap, Larina thought. What do I have to give up now?

"What kind of sacrifice?" Miguel asked.

"Human blood must be traded for the life of the world."

"That doesn't sound so bad, how much?" Miguel tilted his head toward Larina as if asking her to agree.

She laid a hand on his arm, trying to tell him with her touch, not to bargain with the voice. Not to give it leverage.

"All of it. All the blood from the same body."

"Forget it," Larina said.

The laugh that came made the hair rise on the back of her neck. "Self-centered, just like all the others. All the blood from one body, or some of the blood from all the bodies. Your choice. What's the world worth to you?" She could tell the voice enjoyed spreading misery. What was up with that?

"What does he look like?" Could it be someone she knew?

Miguel squinted into the middle distance. "Kinda average," he said. "Medium build, medium height, brownish hair, brownish eyes, tan or Hispanic, like he's trying to blend the most average attributes of any person." He shook his head. "I don't think he has an actual form. If he does he's trying to hide it. Do we scare you, shadow-man?"

"Careful," Larina whispered, feeling electricity on her skin as if before a lightning strike. Power gathered around them, preparing for use. She pulled Miguel to the side, just as the force slammed into her solar plexus. All the breath left her body and her heart stopped.

"Larina!" Miguel caught her as she slid to the floor. "She can't breathe."

The bartender ran out and applied the Heimlich maneuver to her gut. The action started her heart, and her lungs began taking in air.

"Ow!"

"You're okay." Miguel hugged her. His arms were those of a grown man and his chest lay hard and solid against her ear.

"We have to get out of here," she gasped.

Miguel handed his credit card to the bartender. "We're leaving."

"Where to?" he asked as they got into the convertible. "What's your address?"

"I need to go to the Crystal Aura."

"I thought you didn't start work until three."

"I need to get there." She shrugged unable to give an explanation.

"You can't change anything." The voice had a hard sound.

"Back off." Miguel waved it off.

Larina sank into the high-quality leather seats. She watched as Miguel keyed in the code to start the engine. The car roared out of the lot and down Paradise to Sahara. They passed the Stratosphere and kept going. The bungie jumpers' screams filled with terror as if they knew their time was up.

"You can't change anything. You had a chance, but you lost it."

"Miguel-" she started.

"I heard." He pushed the car through a red light. Brakes squealed, and horns trumpeted in anger. They passed the Golden Steer, and the life-sized head turned to watch them. The Flight of the Valkyries started to play on the radio.

Larina hit the tuner, but the music refused to change. She switched the radio off to no effect. The music roared out of the speakers unimpeded. She pulled her I-Pod out and plugged it in. Night on Bald Mountain blared.

"You think that's better?" Miguel didn't take his eyes off the road, but the sarcasm rolled off him like angry cologne.

"I didn't choose it," she said, her fingers pressing everywhere on the I-Pod looking to turn it off. "I can't believe this," she screamed, and the speaker boomed out I'm a Believer sung by Smash Mouth.

They sped past Decatur, then Jones. "Turn here!" she yelled.

Miguel spun the wheel and skidded sideways into the strip mall.

She unsnapped her seatbelt and ran toward the

entrance of the Crystal Aura. Halfway there, Miguel yelled and she spun around in time to see him cutting at the webbing of his seatbelt. As he leapt out from behind the wheel, the cut ends snaked after him encircling his arm and jerking him back. He slashed at the belt, and Larina ran toward him nail scissors in hand. In one smooth motion, she stabbed down into the cushion just behind the hissing buckle. "I call Isis, Mother of the Nile, I call Feya, Mother of fire and I call on Hera the betrayed. Hear me, mothers of gods and mothers of men. Kill this evil intention, deprive it of its unseemly desires and quench its fire. For this I promise you all gifts most worthy."

The writing stopped, along with the music. The only sound in the parking lot was their combined breathing.

Miguel started to laugh. "Nail scissors? You killed it with nail scissors?" The buckle and webbing lay inert with the pink handles of the scissors sticking through them and obscenely into the beautiful leather of the seats.

"Oh Miguel, I am so sorry. I have insurance." She babbled in relief and fear.

"Don't worry, I'm covered."

A sudden crash slammed them into each other, and they scanned the lot looking for the cause. A dark figure rose out of the dumpster beside them. It loomed over their heads. Larina felt Miguel's muscles tense as if to spring.

The figure threw a leg over the side and shimmied down to stand before them. "Spare change?"

Larina put a hand out. "Sir, you have to get out of here. It's dangerous."

"I ain't goin' nowhere."

"You have to," she said, and tried to pull him away from the car. Before she had gone a step, the dumpster began to glow. Smoke billowed out and formed a figure with multiple arms and glowing eyes. Its mouth opened, and down its throat appeared a void, swirling with need and avarice.

"Wait," Miguel said. "I offer you my blood, the sacred blood of a seventh son of a seventh son. Freely offered. Yours for the taking."

The creature reached for him.

"But only if you let the world continue."

The figure stopped as if considering, then shook its head. "I'll take it anyway," it said, and its voice was the voice Larina had heard all along.

"Take my blood then," Larina offered. "My blood is the sacred blood of the first born daughter, of a first born daughter, of a first born daughter. A trinity of power, freely offered, but only if you leave the world alone."

The figure moved toward her and studied her with eyes of fire. It reached a hand out to touch her. She could smell sulfuric smoke and hear the screams of the damned. Crap, crap, crap, she thought, I'm too big a chicken, I know I'll wimp. I just know it. She took a deep breath and tried not to cough as the hand of the demon assumed physical mass and encircled her. Her skinned burned at its touch and she screamed.

Suddenly she was free, and the monster was backing away. "You ain't takin her, asshole." The homeless man beat at the arms with a trash can lid and jabbed it with a piece of wood. "You want the world, you gotta go through me. I am Change, I am Chaos, I am Loki and Coyote." He jabbed with every word. He changed and became another multi-armed form as blue as Vishnu and as calm as Krishna. He danced with the demon. As they moved he chopped off the arms and then the legs and threw them into the dumpster where they dissipated. At last only a small fire burned on the asphalt. The eyes became embers and died.

"Wow," Larina said. "Um, what do we owe you for saving the world?"

His beautiful face smiled at them. "We all save the world. Every day, we agree that the world can exist." He raised his hands in a blessing. "Go forth and create new life. Have children and prosper." Then he vanished.

Miguel took her hand and squeezed it. "Still wanna go for a beer?"

Lake Lahonton

By Patricia Kranish

"Mammoths, ground sloths big as grizzlies, camels, shy spotted cats, shrub oxen with horns that spanned the length of two men, lumbering cave bears, fast horses with delicate hooves, and the dire wolves and sleek lions that ate them, all came to the shores of Lake Lahonton to drink."

The storyteller's dark hair glimmered in the red and yellow light of the fire. She was the youngest daughter of the very old man interred within Spirit Cave. A grandmother herself, in the play of light and shadow, smoke and exhaled breath, her face was young again.

"Where did they go?"

She looked to the wide circle of people, the clans of the four rivers, gathered outside of the cave to honor the old man. His body, swaddled in fur and woven tule, lay within. The living kept their dark eyes on her face and waited for her answer. Her carved bracelets clacked as her hands transcribed the story in the flickering light. Only the very youngest had not heard it, and the oldest among them stopped their chatter to hear her tell it again.

"The water covered the world before the ice ledge lingered and the lake shrunk into itself and the animals disappeared. The glacial rains and snow congregated in the mountains to the north, and in the south, their immense footprints were left in the drying mud. Now they are stones," the storyteller pointed to the boulders along the shore. "They live only in dreams and pictures drawn in hidden caves. And the giant hunters etched into the cracked earth who were sent to look for them did not return.

The storyteller tilted her head so that the black river of her hair flowed to one side. "Listen to the drums."

Her whisper danced across the campground and the people felt the echo in their beating hearts.

"Yes," they said, "tell us the story about the time the mountains of ice walked among us."

"Four rivers fed the lake, once the greatest of inland seas, which is the twin of the sky — gray and blue and black by turns. The mother turned to stone still watches over the children of the ancient Cui-ui eaters, the eaters of cutthroat trout and sweet pine nuts, and bitter lichen, the makers of baskets woven tight as gourds. It is our story to tell before memory shrinks like water on a sun-beaten rock.

"See that stone that leans above the shore, like a grieving woman searching for something she's lost?"

"It's very big," said a young child nestled in his grandmother's arms.

"We were giants before the mountains pushed in from the north. The stones were creatures who fed our strength before they grew tired. They left their bones to taunt us, as punishment for wrongs we had no memory of committing. The wind and the melting ice regarded us as beings of no consequence. It quenched our hearths. The snow fell heavy on the roofs and crushed us as we slept, closing off our breath, obstructing the *shipap*, the place of origins, where we first emerged from deep within the earth.

"The cold gripped us hard and the wind blew without ceasing. The young men were gone for days at a time tracking game they never saw. We subsisted on winter bulbs and wild onion. The hunters returned weary, their muscles cramped and stringy, as their hunger consumed their flesh.

"Except for the few hardy persons who remained outside at night keeping watch, we slept within the shelter of the round houses carved into the frozen rock. Two babies, unable to nurse, died within days of each other. Convulsed by fever, eyes rolled back, their small faces took on a waxy repose and they were gone without a cry. We grieved for these untried spirits. We bore the intolerable sting of winter and watched the water throw up its stones.

"The father of one of the dead ran outside the cave. Cursing, he picked up the heaviest stones and hurled them into the face of the wind. 'Show yourself. Show yourself to me and I will kill you with my bare hands!' The wind, mocked his rage, and the stones fell weakly to the ground, rolling across the landscape like pebbles. Fearing the wind could take greater vengeance still, the people in the cave brought him inside.

"'Your child's tender soul will become a flower of the field in the spring,' they soothed. And some believed it was true."

The storyteller pointed to the immovable star, which shows itself at twilight. The listeners looked up. The sky was the blue that makes you cry for its beauty, just before it darkens and the fires in the vastness high above the mountains ignite to forestall the cold of deep night.

"Our kivas' entrance face north," said a young woman with hair plaited in the manner of the newly married, "even though the coldest wind enters there." She pulled her blanket more tightly around herself. She sat close to the fire and her red cheeks grew redder when she spoke.

"We turn our palms open to the sky in prayer to show we understood the power of the wind," the storyteller continued.

"Still, the wind blew the roofs off and penetrated our shelters. We took refuge in the caves. It followed us. When we left to look for food the wind blew our blankets into the pines and left us naked. We were tossed like dry leaves across the frozen ground. The wind turned our breath to ice. It took the air from us to feed its own greed. What could grow when the wind is so angry? The very young and the very old could not suck life from the whirlwind which waited outside our campsites only to gather force and take us by surprise."

"Did they all die," the child asked.

Rattles mimicked the warning of the snake, the cracking of a branch, the sound of the dying's last breath.

"No, the young and the strong lived, but with no grandfather or grandmother to teach them, no children to make them laugh and bring them hope, they suffered the punishment of the wind; loneliness and dread tore at their spirits. And so it continued, season after season until the clans were scattered across the land, each blaming the other for the wounds they suffered.

"Children had to be lashed to the trunks of the sycamores to keep from joining the sky borne branches.

"Finally, the man called Bear, because of his strength and power, spoke to the people. We will take a child to the high mountain from which the wind is blown."

"To live there?"

"In a way," the storyteller said.

"The wind is hungry," three young people who sat huddled beyond the light of the fire said in unison.

The storyteller nodded to them. "So few survivors could remain in the north. All who lived on the shores of the lake suffered from the bitter cold. When the great animals disappeared, and the promise of spring was not kept, Bear said, 'Should my wife have a child I will offer it to the wind'."

The people loosened their leggings to sit more comfortably on the ground. A few lay on their sides and rested their heads on the crook of an elbow. The fire settled and the smoke dispersed in the waning light.

"Bear was young and in his prime--lean and tall and fearless--kin to the eagle everyone said. He had two children when his first wife died and in the proper time he took another woman who was small and beautiful, as our women tend to be. She was quiet and deferred to Bear in everything and in that she was not like a Fox Clan woman at all. You know what they say, when a Fox woman moves her mouth, we all move.

"The wind was busy destroying all living creatures —
the horse, the camel, the lion, the bear, the deer, the rabbits,
the wolves, the foxes, the people. No animal was too large or
small to escape its ravenous appetite. They all did their best to
accommodate the wind. A shelter carved into the earth, a
hearth in its center, the roof supported by a pole as our spine
holds our head in its proper place, is as warm as a mother's
womb, but the wind tore them open. They built fires and
circled them with rocks. The rocks alone were warmed, and
the people froze. Bear's wife became pregnant with the child
Bear had promised to the wind. It was not a happy event.
There was no one left in the camp who knew how to stop a
pregnancy. She was young and weak, and even babies of the
strong succumbed to the cold and harsh weather. And she was
not strong. At first no one noticed that her cycle did not come.
She spoke to no one. Bear, perhaps feeling the life within when
he approached her, knew first. Nevertheless, he said to the
wind, 'spare us and you shall have the child of my wife.' Some
scoffed, 'My child was taken and still the wind blows and
drives the last of our horses scattered bones.'

"Others joined in, 'Does Bear think his child is a more
satisfying meal than all the others the demon wind has
devoured?'

"Bear shook with passion and entreated the wind to

loosen its grip. He trembled and gyrated and hummed. The women of the camp began to dance around him, singing the song for the dead, dancing in circles until they fell to the ground and their eyes rolled back and they shook with the same palsy that afflicted Bear. Now, it was strange that Bear's wife did not shake or sing or fall. She seemed to be trying to become one with the shadows. She stood in the coldest recesses of the camp braced against a tree to keep from getting tossed by the wind. In that bitter cold she didn't move. If her cape slipped off her head she took no notice. When the others, coming back from the nether world of the wind would go and find her, her hair would be frozen, her eyes singed shut by the frost. Yet she endured, and in due time her child was born.

"Winter stayed with them that year. Instead of the tribes of the four rivers coming together to make decisions that affected them all, they waited passively for Bear to engage the wind, to devise a bargain unlike ones they were accustomed to making: 'I will smooth a stone for you to grind seeds and you will give me your fine atlatl. Or I have more fish than my family can eat before they stink, so I will give them to you and one day when you have eaten your fill of the rabbits in your trap by the river, you will share their warm little furs to line my shoes against the wet snow.' A fair trade.

"Bear said, 'I will give you the child and in return you

will not kill us as much.'

"And Bear knew the wind. They all felt the wind, but only he touched it and spoke to it. And it spoke to him. To see him communicate with the wind, I dare not say as an equal, struck them all with wonder."

"Did you see him with your own eyes?" the inquisitive child said.

"Not I, but the old man who lies in Spirit Cave told us he saw him many times. Another man, seeing Bear, would certainly die on the spot. And now the old man is joining him."

"Where?"

The storyteller spread her arms and her bracelets slid to her elbows. Everywhere. Nowhere.

"Bear was twice as big as any living man. Have you seen the stone that juts over all the others on our western shore? That is he. And the pictures carved in the western earth? He made them. When he tired of swimming and walked across the lake, his feet touched the bottom. He did not breathe, so that the wind would not be jealous of his breath and snatch it away. He did not eat or drink for many days before. He cut his forehead and rubbed the blood of an eagle into it so that he became the eagle. His voice a caw, the screech of the predator swooping down on its prey. He visited the spirit world and returned. He answered our questions about where our life goes and from where it comes. He knew why a tree dies even as its leaves are green. He...."

The young woman interrupted, "And Bear's wife?"

"The baby was round and rosy and her mother was transformed. She spoke to her as if she was the only one who could understand her. Her breasts filled with nourishment and the child was eager to suck. I tell you it was hard to rip that infant away. Bear was insistent. Many of the women whose children had died as infants wailed in grief. The mother threw herself down, clung to Bear's feet, begged to die in her infant's place, struck herself with rocks, sucked the blood from her wounds and spat it in Bear's face."

"Is this the way the old man told it?"

"No. This is the women's story. He only spoke of her sadness, not of her disturbed spirit. Most of the people, too sick and weary to endure another winter, believed that Bear had interpreted the wind's intentions correctly. If the wind could keep its bargain, then so could they.

"Bear and his brothers approached the woman as she and the baby slept. As they were about to take the child, she woke up and tried with all her strength to hold onto her. How could she? Bear had three living brothers and they overcame her. Her screams shook the sky. No one came to her aid. I asked why when I first heard the story as a child and most say the wind itself held them in place. That and the fear gnawing their empty bellies. The eyes of the witnesses are closed and so few can read the bones they left behind.

"The brothers brought the infant to the top of the mountain and removed her fur wraps. As they did the little thing woke up. She howled at the assault on her skin. You can still hear her cries when the wind blows."

"And the mother?" The young woman persisted.

"When Bear and his brothers returned to camp with the infant's clothing, she was gone. She took blankets and something else, too — Bear's long spear. She traced their footprints to the top of the mountain, but no one saw her ascend."

The woman said, "Did they look for her?"

"It is not told that they did."

"Did the wind keep its promise?"

"Not right away. The following year, when Bear had taken a new wife, the wind's rage abated. Winter still brings its harsh yield, as you well know, its old intensity has dissipated, its hunger sated."

The young woman shivered.

The storyteller asked, "Are you afraid?"

She said, "I'm puzzled. Men and women have made a bargain too. Women endure the pain of bearing children, while men promise to protect them even if they trade their own lives in the process. Didn't Bear break his promise to the mother? Did he offer the wind his own life as a sacrifice?"

A young man, a distant relative to the old man dead inside Spirit Cave, said, "You make my head hurt with your questions. Be satisfied that the wind doesn't kill you when you're alone and the mountains shake. Be grateful that Bear lived to have many children. If the wind was not appeased, would any of us be alive?"

But of course people who make their homes on mountains can't stop asking questions and arguing with the answer. What happened to the woman after she took Bear's spear? Did she reach her child before the wind devoured her? Why did she take the long spear with her? Why not his atlatl, the superior, lighter, smaller, weapon? Would the wind grow hungry again?

While it was true that the people of the north flourished since that time, the people of the south had diminished to less than five bands living in the place fed by the river that flowed north. Didn't they still say we are like the fingers on one hand? Survival depended on the help of other people. Children were cherished and protected. Mothers could nurse two infants at a time so that a child who survived his mother would not starve. It was in no one's interest to weaken a nursing mother or to sacrifice a healthy child. Live to mourn your parents, that was their hope.

There were stories of distant tribes who lost so many members that even their ability to hunt and make clothing, to build shelters and make fires, was lost. They lay on the ground unable to remember why they were alive in the first place, until the last person died.

"Good story," someone said and while they had gathered for the interment of the old man, it was now time to eat. The beaver, the bear, the deer, the rabbit, even a slow and aging wolf, went into the pot. The children, many who never saw each other before, fell into immediate and exuberant play as if they had made plans for this time together before they were born. The girls took each other's hands to form circles for their games while the boys broke through, and churned the ground with their sturdy legs. They leapt and tumbled as though the rocks and frozen earth were cushioned with feathers. The fatigue they complained of on the long trek to Spirit Cave evaporated at the sight of other children spinning and screeching in the eternal language of child play.

The adults, who called the other clans howlers, squabblers, rabbit-killers and locust-eaters (and worse when they were not in each other's presence) told stories where they were swift, clever and brave. And the listeners never tired of hearing them.

"Oh," they would exclaim, "did you hear how far Wolf Moon claimed he threw his spear? It went through North Star's heart before striking the deer."

As the story was repeated, the teller became a witness, "I did see it!" And the spear became a shooting star. "It hasn't landed yet!"

The excitement of the farthest, the biggest, and the strongest lifted their spirits high above the solid ground that held them fast. The dusty road across the sky that the old man would soon travel would welcome them all. And the lake that overflowed with tears would always feed them forever.

Aleatory Nevada

By Jay Hill

Sara Emanon lives in a stormwater tunnel linking northwest urbanized Clark County to a large detention basin. The tunnel is part of a $2 billion, 250-mile system of tunnels designed to reduce flooding in Las Vegas. Rain is rare in the Mojave and, most of the year, the tunnels remain dry. More than 1,000 homeless use them for shelter.

The tunnels are constructed from pre-cast concrete pieces. Some are large enough to accommodate two pickup trucks with room to spare. They are dark and sooty, a favorite of scorpions and there's a constant odor of cigarette smoke and urine. The homeless outfit their squats with mattresses, tables, coolers, camp lights, candles, stolen port-a-potties and water jugs. When rains come, everything is washed away, including people who fail to get out.

The habitués of the tunnels are a shadow people, the semi-invisibles of a culture: freaks, misfits, outcasts, dreamers, bullshit artists, Ginsburgian poets and preachers, druggies, alcoholics, gambling addicts, PTSD vets, immigrants, hiders, seekers, the wanted, the unwanted, the exiled, the economically challenged and the abandoned. They are translucent ghosts, ignored, willfully unseen, looked through and, when their existence becomes undeniable, treated as an uncomfortable, unwelcome presence; undesirable strangers in their own land. They can create something from nothing and refuse anything from anyone. Some are proud beggars and some are not.

The tunnel dwellers live with cement skies, black nights and echoes of madness. They drown in flash floods; new age, post-modern victims of a gentler, kinder nation. Objects of scorn, wrath and rage, they have shortened lifespans and a surplus of illness. Some are long suffering and some are afflicted with impulsive, explosive anger. They are heroes and villains, saints and felons, tolerant and intolerant, mostly alone and lonely; doomed by off-putting, Pekarian neuroses. They are bonded to loneliness, despair and depression by emotional glue that strengthens with age.

Sara squats in a short spur that was used as a tool shed during the tunnel's construction. Plans called for the spur to be sealed, but it had been forgotten, or ignored, and remained open. Sara uses the space as her live-in studio. She keeps some canvases there, but moves older pieces to her half-sister's barn in Pahrump.

Abe Ramen was thinking about Sara again. Abe knew Sara to be a generous painter with grubby moles and fragile, multi-colored fingers. Sara once proclaimed to Abe, "I'm the world's greatest thermo-petrol visual artist." Abe did not understand what Sara meant and told himself that he had no interest in learning her other colors.

Abe thinks he knows the secret to life. He loves arid Las Vegas and the drab, deafening desert. He hears the Joshua trees burning. He feels the boulders hold down the landscape. He listens to the sagebrush taunt the wind. The desert talks to him like no one else. He alone is the holder of its secrets. The Strip casinos feed his anger and whisper messages to him. Abe hears the sky roar with delight because it has trapped the sun. He walks to a window; his aluminum shirt reflects the landscape. Abe knows the horizon is envious of the images he holds in his eyes.

Abe sees something move in the distance. It is the approaching figure of Sara. Abe gulps. Sara and her studio rush toward him, envelope him and he is inside them. Sara's brain tastes of mauve and lemon, it is cool like a 1970's kitchen appliance. Abe thinks it may be a refrigerator.

Abe sees his reflection in a mirror. The images Abe projects from his mind, those of the Mojave and Sara's studio, form transient patterns, a world more immediate and more in the present than the physical world. The images become a cinematic synthesis of Abe's emotions and life. Abe experiences a rare moment of peace.

Abe is a patient coward, a survivor and a brandy drinker. He has a pointed head and fungal fingernails. His friends believe him to be an unclean, craven poll worker, a sycophantic, patronage beneficiary. Abe believes he once saved a death crone and is proud of it, but Abe's patience, fantasy heroism and fungal fingers are not sufficient for what he believes Sara wants. Abe runs away.

Abe looks up and sees the sun is a talking guppy with the taste of asparagus and the fire of pansies. He feels separated, isolated and excluded. "You can't bully me," he yells at the sun. Abe begins to walk with an exaggerated swagger. He picks up a piece of chewing gum that has been spit on the sidewalk and massages it with his fingers. When the gum asks for a happy ending, Abe sees remorse and disgust as yellow and black. He throws the gum down a sewer drain.

Abe steps inside. He is in Sara's studio again. Sara comes closer. Abe sees lonely knives fly from her eyes. Abe's heart is wounded. It becomes a blue snake and eats his soul. Abe feels secure. Without a soul, he cannot be harmed.

Sara glares at Abe with the wrath of a repulsive rat. She says, in a hushed voice, with the sour anger of a squeezed lemon, "I hate you, Abe. - I demand sacrifice."

Abe studies Sara's grubby, hairy moles and her fragile, colored fingers. He takes a deep breath. "I'm sorry," Abe begins, in an apologetic tone, "but I don't feel the same. I never will. I don't hate you Sara, but I accept and validate your hate for me. It's the only thing in my life that makes sense and gives me purpose."

Abe travels back to an earlier time, considers that he is more lonely in the past than in the present. He returns to the present and fingers the minuscule gun he has hanging in his pierced left earlobe. "Sara, I love you," he continues.

Sara says, "You haven't stopped."

Sara looks at Abe with anxiety. Abe imagines she is a hollow, hungry hamster being cooked over coals at a stingy wedding; a wedding with recorded classical music and two spiteful Uncle's dressed as Capuchin monks gyrating to a distorted Samba rhythm. Sara is jumpy, her emotions rubbed raw like a strung-out map in need of a fix. Sara's right hand is water-boarded on a craps table in the desert beneath a mourning moon. Abe sees Sara's liver shatter into 38 rectangles: 18 red, 18 black and 2 green. Abe puts his money on even.

Sara's half-sister takes her to visit their mother in Philadelphia. Sara is drawn away into the distance; a long, slow magnetic disappearance, like a train in a neorealist film.

With Sara gone, Abe acts to meet her demand. He goes to Sara's studio and loads her canvasses into a white Dodge dually. He drives 500 miles north, to the Black Rock Desert, the Burning Man Event, throws the canvasses into a bonfire stack and watches them burn.

When Sara returns she files a complaint with, what she calls, "the prostitutor's office." The Clark County DA prosecutes Abe in a highly publicized trial. Abe's oldest son, an Army officer, is granted compassionate leave to attend the trial. At Abe's request, a wax figure of Princess Di is brought from a Strip museum and placed beside him. Former news presenters and disgraced celebrity poker players swarm the trial in the hope that they will be interviewed. Two Fremont Street performance artists are refused entry when they appear in American flag themed thongs and pasties, but two other performers are admitted, one costumed as the Jack of Hearts and the other as a Sponge Bob Dylan.

Sara refuses to testify against Abe, but she delivers a didactic lecture on the persecution and oppression of artists in

American culture, telling the Judge that the courts operate to place an imprimatur of legitimacy on the poor taste of the ruling class and that her paintings were stolen and destroyed by former President Jimmy Carter in retaliation for Sara's interference in Carter's efforts to negotiate the terms of a cease-fire between the Encore and the Wynn. Sara says that Abe did her a favor by destroying her art, which she describes as insipid, turgid trash that only a lawyer could love.

Sara begs the Judge to acquit Abe. The Judge, hidden behind her podium, with only her head and part of her upper body visible, clenches a .38 revolver in her right hand. She fears everyone in the courtroom, believing they are psychotic, pixilated or somewhere in between.

The DA makes his case using tapes of Sara's initial interview, the affidavit filed with her complaint, her testimony before the grand jury and CCTV footage of Abe removing Sara's paintings and loading them into the pickup truck. The DA presents a Burning Man Event recording of Abe pitching Sara's paintings into a bonfire while dressed in an offensive Native American costume, dancing a jig and drinking from a bottle of Irish whiskey.

Abe, against the advice of his attorney and, ignoring the cautions of the Judge, insists on testifying. On the witness stand, Abe, refers to himself as "The Savonarola of Las Vegas," testifies to every fact necessary for his conviction, ecstatically taking credit for the destruction of Sara's paintings. Abe begins with a lucid, rational, chronological description of the events, but soon his testimony becomes emotional and irrational. Abe tells the Judge that the spirit of Richard Feynman has been transmogrified into LSD and that it is being held by the government in Area 51 inside a Chanel No. 5 bottle in the glove box of a 1949 Hudson Commodore. Abe claims that he can channel Feynman's spirit.

Abe begins speaking in a high-pitched, lilting voice, which he says is Feynman's. Abe tells the Judge that she has no authority to convict polymers, acrylics, or synethesiatics of felonies of high art, claiming that the right do so is reserved exclusively to direct descendants of the Biblical Philistines. The Judge warns Abe that he is under oath, but Abe continues. He testifies that the Philistines have given him transactional immunity from prosecution. Abe produces a document from his vest pocket, says that it is his immunity grant and begins to read it. Abe's recitation is soon recognized by the court clerk (though not the judge, because she has never read anything other than trashy, fantasy, romance-bondage novels) as a mangled paraphrase of John Keats's Ode to a Nightingale.

The Judge ignores Sara's request to acquit Abe. The Judge convicts everyone, that being the politically safe thing to do. She finds Abe guilty of felony vandalism. Upon hearing the verdict, Abe tells the Judge his crimes are artistic. He calls the Judge an ignorant clucking dung beetle and tells her that she is a container of quantum ignorance. The Judge tells Abe that if she didn't think he was crazy she would hold him in contempt. Abe's attorney moves for a verdict of not guilty by reason of insanity. The Judge denies the motion and explains that, while she thinks Abe's behavior is the product of some mental defect and he may not responsible for his courtroom behavior, she believes Abe knew that what he did was wrong and that Abe could not meet the tests of the M'Naghten Rule. Abe interrupts the Judge and informs her that he has found her guilty by reason of sanity in accordance with The Rule in the McWhopper-New Coke Case.

Abe's bond is revoked and he is ordered held in the Clark County Detention Center (CCDC) pending sentencing. Abe understands none of this and tells a courtroom deputy that he has a pipeline to God's rectum. The deputy tells Abe that Abe will be with people who share the same pipeline. As he is led away, Abe yells at the judge that she may imprison his corporeal essence, but he will be vacationing in the Mirage and swimming with dolphins. The Judge tells Abe that she is both happy and sad for him.

Publicity from the trial enables Sara to sell her remaining art at ridiculous prices to art slumming Hollywood scum. At their next cocktail party, the scum show their slime friends that they own a piece of Sara's art and then, after snorting large quantities of cocaine, the scum and the slime burn Sara's art and celebrate the triumph of Abe.

While awaiting sentencing Abe and Sara are married. Abe wants to dress as Elvis for the ceremony, but the jail administrator refuses Abe's request and he is married in an orange CCDC jumpsuit. Sara wears a Xena: Warrior Princess costume. Their ceremony is performed by a Rastafarian priest who uses a faux blunt and blesses the newlyweds with a sprinkling of organic oregano from the CCDC kitchen.

At Abe's sentencing, Sara pleads for mercy. She attempts to explain the Butterfly Theory. In a rambling, incoherent speech, she asserts that free will does not exist. Sara, lost and confused in her own thoughts, tells the Judge that it doesn't matter what the Judge will do because whatever the Judge does is something that was predetermined at the time of the big bang or, maybe, the big band era. Sara admits that she is not sure at which time it was predetermined or if it makes any difference because each and every moment is totally dependent on each and every other moment. Sara says she may not have any idea what she is saying or if she knows what predetermined means or if anything could change the moment she is having because it must be as it is.

Predictably unmoved, the judge sentences Abe to 1 year and 1 day in prison. Sara visits Abe at every opportunity. She begins to call herself Sonia and refers to Abe as Dimitri. In prison, Abe hand duplicates Dostoevsky's Notes From a Dead House.

Upon his release, Abe tries to have his hand written, plagiarized manuscript published as his own work. It is repeatedly rejected for publication. Abe receives scathing letters from editors. They uniformly criticize his story for poor plotting and lack of literary merit and suggest that Abe take their proprietary writing course. After many submissions, one editor recognizes Abe's manuscript for what it is. Abe becomes a pariah in the publishing industry.

With his attempt to become a published writer through plagiarism derailed, Abe spray paints a sign outside his cardboard box shelter which, among other things, claims he is "The World's Greatest Lawyer." Abe attracts, as his first client, a fellow tunnel dweller who has been charged with vagrancy. Abe files a legalistic-sounding motion to dismiss the charge against his client based on the "preposition" that his client is not a resident of the planet earth and demanding "trail" by jury. When Abe appears in court to argue the motion, he is arrested and charged with the unauthorized practice of law. Abe becomes a hero to the tunnel dwellers and is swamped with clients.

For Abe's trial, Sara paints a large paper triptych. It depicts Jesus, with the face of Abe, as an infant, in the wilderness and crucified. Sara folds the triptych and hides it in her purse. During the testimony of the prosecution's first witness, Sara stands, unfolds triptych and displays it to the Court and gallery, shouting, "Justice is not legal. This man murders art."

The Judge orders Sara removed from the courtroom. Before a bailiff can reach her, Sara produces a deck of Tarot cards from her purse, throws them in the air and screams, "I have the courage of a radish!" The judge orders Sara brought before her and demands that Sara apologize to the Court, and the gallery, for her behavior. Sara tells the Judge that she would rather kiss a smelly water cooler scorpion than respect a flea. The Judge thinks Sara's statement is a disguised, metaphoric, Freudian sexual insult and sentences Sara to three days for contempt of court. At CCDC intake, a social worker evaluates Sara, concludes Sara is schizophrenic and has her placed on a psych hold. Sara is transferred to a mental health facility where she is disruptive, sedated with Thorazine and released after three days.

Abe is convicted of the unauthorized practice of law. The Judge, seeing that Abe has done no economic harm to the legal community (because Abe's client couldn't pay a lawyer), sentences Abe to no jail time, but orders Abe to perform 16 hours of community service. Abe tells the Judge, "I'll suck rhinoceros snot out of a porcupine's butt before I do that." The Judge, tired of the Abe and Sara show, orders the clerk to call the next case.

Sara's release is celebrated by everyone in the stormwater community except Abe who has become fearful that Sara will murder him as a sacrifice to appease, Albert Einstein who Abe has concluded is Sara's relative. That night a full glass of brandy could not calm Abe's nerves.

At the celebration, held on a discarded craps table, using plastic cups and stolen liquor, Abe takes a long swallow of brandy, looks up and sees the stars and four moons that Sara has painted on the ceiling of the tunnel. Abe sees them as vanilla ice cream and chocolate syrup. He says, "I know the sacrifice of Art for Godot and why numbers are colored."

"Abe did it all for me," Sara tells everyone, "I don't know how anyone could endure such pain, but he did, and he did it for me."

"It was easy," Abe tells Sara, "I am the E.E. Cummings of Bunkerville and the Hemingway of the Mojave. I am an artist who has fallen among legalisms. For you, I will be stoned in the desert." Abe produces a joint and starts toward an exit.

"Abe, you're my hero," Sarah calls to him, "my one and only one, well maybe, at least today or in the moment that's passing - unless it's already gone forever."

Who Sits at the Left Hand of God?

By Carole McKinnis

On a moist November morning, I was awake, a strong cup of coffee in hand. Storms in Mexico were sending rain and wind into the desert. I watched through the window of my music room. The fall leaves on the peach orchard were a bright cascade of orange and gold. Defying the dark skies, wind, and rain, the trees lit up the yard. The leaves clung to the branches, too brilliant and enthusiastic to fall. Peaches do well in Las Vegas, if you feed and water them.

I stood by my ancient Steinway gazing out at the work of wind and rain on our little orchard. I balanced my coffee cup on an old copy of Handel's "Messiah" sitting on the piano's lowered protective lid. Before students began to arrive, my own lesson for the day was to work through a few small, challenging credenzas in a Mozart aria. Morning coffee enhances my willingness to work. Diminishes the voice a little, but that disappears as I practice. I needed to quit watching the "Nature taking on my Orchard" show and get busy.

The door-bell rang. Eleanor Standish stood there in a swivet. A tall, blonde woman, she wore a caped, black and red ensemble. The outfit was just theatrical enough to make the swivet seem important.

Eleanor is an international conductor/musician, greatly recognized all over Las Vegas, and as a result, always over-scheduled. Eleanor is also one of the decision makers for the musical department at UNLV. Originally, the university acquired her as a skilled teacher of piano and organ. She conducts endless, busy groups in all musical venues. Every musician in Las Vegas knows her. Besides all the public recognition, she is my favorite piano accompanist. I am part of why she is over-scheduled. She stood before me in the rainy wind, carrying a zipped tote-bag full of unsung music.

"Celeste! Urraca Feraz has the *flu!*"

Not sure what I was supposed to do with that. I've never liked the flamboyant Urraca, flamboyance being no substitute for talent. Even so, I wouldn't wish her a good case of flu. Why bother?

"And...?" I queried.

"She won't be able to do the Vivaldi oratorio! I'm hoping you'll do those for me."

"Why didn't you just call me to do it in the first place?" I asked.

"Oh, you know how Urraca is! She loves to impress everyone, get the publicity, but she doesn't like to spend time doing the work. The Feraz's are the primary financial supporters of the music program. I don't want to make an enemy of Urraca. It's so easy to just give her the part and then let her walk away when she gets bored. And that never seems to take long."

"So wonderful to be asked to substitute for the brilliant, wealthy Urraca!" I said. "People will naturally think I was second choice."

Eleanor was shocked. "*You*? Second to Urraca Feraz? Never! Celeste, I *need* you!"

Well, that helped, some. And how could I say no to a woman who anticipated my every need for breathing space?

We spent the next hour working on the "Domine Deus", "Qui Sedes" and the duet. I love to sing with Eleanor's – well, let's say it – her *second-best* soprano, Suzanne Swinford. I smirked over that. No doubt Suzanne would kindly describe *me* the same way. So many times, after singing together, audience members paid the odd compliment that our intertwined voices sounded like one.

Eleanor energetically scribbled her musical expectations for me on the University's copy of Vivaldi's "Gloria". So many of these obscured Vivaldi's elegant Italian preferences. Naturally, I would read both versions and decide which I liked better.

As Eleanor packed up to leave, my ten o'clock student, Mikael Strauss was at the door. Mikael is a beautiful singer, beyond what I've taught him, some day he'll be a very well known singer. A gorgeous young Argentine man, over six feet tall, curly bronze hair. A glorious tribute to his grand-father, a German officer who left World War II in a timely way. Mikael's voice carried the high clear notes of a Wagnerian Heldentenor, but he could also manage the soft subtleties of the Italian composers. A tremendous range. His voice easily slipped into the darker baritone notes, keeping the same clarity across the tessitura. I *should* give him up to Doctor Hoffman, but I love his voice. All of Dr. Hoffman's tenors sound alike.

Mikael likes the climb to my house on the western hills of Las Vegas. It's quiet here. He can work, undisturbed by the distractions of the campus. Besides my own, more sophisticated view of the singer's world, he loves my oatmeal cookies.

Repacking her tote bag to leave, Eleanor suddenly

focused on Mikael.

"Mikael! Why are you not in "The Gloria" rehearsals?"

"I thought that was for girls." he answered.

"No! No!" Eleanor struggled, stuffing music into her bag, "There are several areas where we need solid tenors…please come out the minute you can. Celeste will prepare you!"

I handed Eleanor her dainty, two-tailed Mermaid cup, which I'd refilled with better coffee, and gave her a little bag of home-made oatmeal cookies.

"Oh, Good! Now I won't have to stop before I get to the Smith Center!" An elegant swirl of the black and red cape and she was off to the next of her scheduled crescendos.

Mikael and I allowed the drapes to re-settle themselves after Eleanor's whirl-wind departure.

"She's really quick to rope a person in, isn't she?" Mikael said.

"She is, but she is *so* worth it! She's gotten you a couple of grants, hasn't she?"

He laughed. "I appreciate everything she does. But we must be ready for her sudden calls to action. By the way, this IS Vivaldi, isn't it? There *are* lots of girls, aren't there?"

"So many!" I assured him, as I flipped through *"The Gloria"* to find the good Tenor lead-ins.

For the next week and a half I worked on the Vivaldi. Mikael showed up with two more tenors. Close friends who worked in one of the popular "Retro" shows. One played the role of Frank Sinatra, the other one, Dean Martin.

Meetings with Suzanne Swinford, Eleanor playing piano. Finally the rehearsal with the full orchestra.

I have sung in many productions with Eleanor's preferred oboist, Emile Lanier. A quiet man, in spite of many offers to play around the world, he chose to work in several of the large casino orchestras. His day job kept him busy in the electronics department of a radio station. A slightly built, somewhat stoop-shouldered man, Emile seemed to have a case of the traditional Las Vegas flu that we get in the fall. His performance was light and punctual, but with none of his usual style and panache. Several busy Las Vegans had ignored this particular flu. A surprising number of them were dead.

Even in bad health, Emile's precise performance was worth hearing. During this last practice, as I was supposed to enter on the "Domine Deus". I confidently opened my mouth, and nothing came out. I waved to Eleanor. Batting her baton on the dais, she halted the orchestra.

"What's the problem, Celeste?"

"Sorry, I'm having a slight glitch in my throat. A little water and I'll be fine."

I sipped from my Evian bottle and the entrance began again. No trouble. It worried me, though. I never miss an entrance. Usually, I never miss an entrance.

Leaving rehearsal, I wrapped my throat in my Pashmina scarf before I put on my coat. At home I made a pot of tea and drank it with lemon and honey…and a little rum. I *did not* have a problem, and I wanted to make sure things stayed that way.

Friday. Performance at seven p.m. The theater offered good seating for a thousand people. The acoustics were pretty good.

I did light rehearsals. Especially for the entrance to "Domine Deus". A light run-through for "Laudamus Te". No fears there. If I missed anything in the duet, I could count on Suzanne Swinford to effortlessly sing both parts. What are friends for?

She looked divine in her burnt-orange velvet gown, a perfect complement to her auburn hair, though the scoop neck was a bit low cut. I wore a burgundy velvet gown, my favorite color, since it showcased my copper curls. Admittedly, my dress was cut as low as Suzanne's, but I have the generous décolletage to pull it off. Poor Suzanne was just trying to keep up.

All the preparation and then, through the doors to this great-spirited Mass, *"The Vivaldi Gloria."*

The great opening, full of off-beats, back-beats and the heart-tearing beauty of world class tenors, Mikael Strauss laying it all out, with his two friends for the fourteen man tenor section. So glorious, I almost wished I were just sitting to hear it all myself. Almost.

In the "Laudamus Te", Suzanne and I were glorious, I admit it. Though I longed for a sip of water, but I was well prepared for the entrance to "Domine Deus".

Obviously, Emile Lanier felt much better. The yearning plangency of the oboe made it's heaven-soaring ascent. Emile Lanier provided a high-tension energy to the part. The section played on, both mortal and heavenly. Glorious to hear. My entrance arrived.

I did not. My mouth opened, my will was there, but nothing came out. I froze.

With no hesitation, Emile nodded briefly to Eleanor and then launched into an instantly re-imagined riff of what he'd just played. Pure Vivaldi. Pure Emile. Emile and Vivaldi rising. The melody rose over fields and forests; sun and rain, rejoicing. The orchestra was silent. Emile and Vivaldi cast vivacious waterfalls of music. Soaring golden leaves of purest light. In some timeless moment, nodding again to Eleanor,

Emile came gently back to my entrance. I entered, perfectly, of course, carried on the waves of what this True Musician had created.

I have never sung better.

The whole ensemble was transformed. We reached the finale, *"Gloria."* The tenors and basses were Thrones and Virtues of leading angels, the sopranos and contraltos rejoicing over the top of the deeper voices.

The audience was on its feet applauding until their hands were tired, and then they applauded some more. I looked around to see where Emile was and couldn't find him.

Suzanne and I took several bows. We were swept up and away from the theater by Mikael and his two bravos. I knew I would see Emile at the Pepper Mill of the Gods. What would I do when I saw him? Bending him over backwards in a big smooch would be crass, but it seemed appropriate.

More acceptable at the bar, than at the presentation.

Emile wasn't there. In all the festivity, I decided I'd call him tomorrow.

Emergencies kept the next couple of days busy. Mikael had a chance to go with the two Sinatra and Dean Martin improvs to Los Angeles. They wanted to try out for the three young artists voices in La Traviata. I worked with them. Considering what the two improv-twins were getting for their regular jobs, they didn't need the money, they just wanted to take a run at it.

Sunday, I sang four services. Different denominations. My own way of "Staying Good" with God.

Monday morning, the faithful Steinway waited patiently. I needed more time with my coffee. Let Mozart *try* to take me on after Friday's performance! Just a moment with the last of the coffee and the morning's paper. Leafing through to the cross-words I noticed the obituary column,

A friend had found Emile Lanier dead at his home, Sunday morning. My day stopped. Then restarted.

I called the lady. She said he'd been tired after *"The Gloria."* He went home and died sometime in the night.

I couldn't grasp it. The lyrics from "The Gloria" came and went. *"Qui Sedes?" "Who sits on the Right Hand of God?"* Well, that was traditionally established. At the left hand of God a quiet man stands, the clever hands at ease with the oboe. Set free, he lets his soul make great musical riffs of hope and joy. He throws vibrant longing into the eternal air of Eden at the end of summer, when the leaves fall.

I sat for a while longer. The coffee cooling in my cup. Mexico sending storms into the desert. A cold wind brought rain into the peach orchard. Fewer leaves now, deep in November. A sudden gust tore small golden sigils off the trees. Exuberantly they unraveled, twirling away over desert pines and houses like mysterious, piercing notes from some divinely inspired oboe; the subtle falls of sound, the soaring ascents.

While the wind tore away the glittering leaves, I could hear all of it clearly.

Oracle in a Red Coat

By Karen Bryant

When I was eight, I learned a big word -- chaos. Not from the dictionary. I breathed it in, felt it inside my body, survived it.

My first teacher -- mother's cancer; daily lessons. The second -- dad's suitcase; forever. Then, coloring books in waiting rooms, smiling therapists asking me questions I didn't understand, pills to "help me concentrate."

When I was nine, I saw a butterfly on the cover of my mother's *Scientific American* in the bathroom, opened it up and found an explanation of it all. A butterfly flaps its wings over Brazil; a tornado erupts in Texas. It was about weather systems, but I saw the larger implications; the impact of small changes. Chaos. From that day forward I kept one foot in what was and another in what could be and waited to be ripped apart. It took twenty years, but it happened. It always happens.

One cold desert day in February, I was crouching behind the Acacia bush outside the garage of my rented two-bedroom house a stone's throw off the Strip *(the equivalent of the wrong side of the glitzy tracks)*, brushing aside the small pebbles to make a flat surface on which to place my new ceramic Buddha. I had just bought him at a stand in front of the abandoned gas station down the street, marked down from $29.99 to $12.99. *Times are bad when even Buddha isn't holding his value.* I had to wonder if a discounted idol might have diminished powers. But I was under pressure to make some fast changes in my life, so I plopped down the money and stuck him under my arm. It was a small act, not nearly as grand as a butterfly flap, but I hoped that the mere presence of this smiling icon might shift the energy in my miserable life and inspire me to find a little peace.

On that fateful day, I was looking for just the right spot for Buddha so he might set the tone for my day, someplace where I'd pass him every morning as I backed out of my garage on my way to my job at the Pleasure Palace. The Pleasure Palace—a misnomer of grand proportions. I don't tell everyone this, but I used to work for a sex toy supply house in the grittier part of Las Vegas. I stocked the shelves in the warehouse and on my breaks I scribbled spoof ads hocking the dildos and vibrators that filled the warehouse shelves. My boss Martha, always in a skirt, blouse and sensible shoes, snooped and was captivated. She said I had talent and maybe I could make our quarterly 25-page catalog pulsate. I was stoked that someone thought my scribblings were worth something. Of course, I still had to work my shift in the warehouse.

How about this one for The Starter Kit, item # 269 on page 5? *Be the woman you always knew you were and he always hoped you'd become with the Lady Splendor neon blue wig, personal hand-stitched leather whip and erotic rhythmic CD. Pure pleasure unzipped for just $79.99.* It started to sell big time and my writing career was off and running.

Truth was, I found no pleasure working at the Pleasure Palace. I was the only guy in an estrogen-infused group of graphic designers, middle managers and "administrative assistants" whose sole focus was to meet deadlines, increase profits and improve "their little fellow" — me.

Shashaunna, one of my colleagues, was the inspiration for Buddha in a round-about way. After listening patiently to my tirade about the job, my mother and life in general, she smiled at me, head shaking teacher-like, nose ring glittering in the florescent light, blue hair spiking out from a short bleached cut, and said, "Blaise," *(she christened me Blaise since Jonathan was just too plain for the shining spirit that lurks deep within me),* "you need an attitude adjustment, dude. You're bringing us all down. How can you write such gleeful fuck-copy yet be a constant source of gloom?" Even with her short stature and tattooed arms, when she spoke she commanded attention.

I had no idea how to manifest this attitude adjustment. So, when I saw the fattest Buddha I had ever seen on my way to snag some cigs, I thought, "Why not?" That's how I ended up behind the bush, jimmying the fat guy into the hard dirt under the pebbles, planting new hope for salvation.

So you can see, I wasn't hiding, intentionally. But when the woman in the red coat walked by that chilly afternoon, I'm sure she couldn't see me. And I couldn't see her, at least not the first time. I heard her, however. Just one fragmented phrase — *unknowable connections*. It dropped like a wadded up $5 bill falling accidentally out of God's pocket, like mad money from Heaven. She kept right on going, unaware that anyone had heard her.

I peeked around the bush, but all I could see was a red coat lumbering down the street walking a dog, or was the dog walking the coat? The coat was going at a fast clip to keep up with the canine – breed unknown at that point.

I admit that at the onset, I had no idea of the value of those words, but I sensed I'd use them one day; they were too good to waste. And they definitely fit my world view. At that moment, however, it just seemed weird. And, there was Buddha smirking at me, like he wasn't surprised, like he knew what was starting. He was turning out to be just one more mocking face to irritate the hell out of me.

I went inside and wrote her words on a Post-It— *unknowable connections* —and stuck in on the refrigerator. I didn't know then how that phrase and its source would eventually stir the deepest part of my psyche. Now, with all that has transpired, I remember that first message as the beginning of the most profound one-way conversation I have ever had. More meaningful than my nightly childhood prayers to God, whom I never saw nor heard, nor, for that fact, knew if he was really there.

The next morning, I drove out of the garage with purpose. I would stare down the little fat guy and not be intimidated or beguiled. Maybe Buddha's silent message had worked for others for millennia, but his "just be" attitude was already starting to irritate me.

The drive to work was pretty standard. Cursing at red lights, at cars merging in front of me, at a man I almost hit as he dashed across the street for the bus. "What the fuck? Asshole! Why me, God?"

As though answering my own foolish question, *unknowable connections* floated up and spread itself across my windshield and stopped me cold. Suddenly, I saw each one of those irritating beings with their own story swirling about them. Maybe they were as miserable as I was. Maybe they were also hurtling to jobs they hated, living lives nowhere near as fulfilling as they had hoped for.

For a millisecond I wasn't sure where I ended and those people out there began. *Unknowable connections.* The words seeped in and filled my gaps like putty, providing a few moments of serenity. And then my daily soundtrack turned itself on full blast: *What am I doing? Where is my life going? Is there anyone out there who will love me? Love me? Hell, will I ever get laid? Or, am I doomed to wander the earth writing about sex toys and erotic secrets with no one to share it all with?*

At the end of the day, I pulled into my driveway, bored, hungry, thirsty. There he sat, waiting for me with the patience only a Buddha could muster. I couldn't help but look upon his rotund exterior and think, *you must live on a steady diet of fast food to be that fat. What do you have to smile about?* I was kneeling down to pick him up and drop him in the trash can when I heard a scuffling sound. Before I had a chance to turn around, another phrase dropped. *I told you so!* It was her. Walking her dog; lobbing another disconnected phrase, this time like a grenade. And right at my driveway again — same time as yesterday. *I told you so!* And then she was gone. Who was she talking to? What wisdom did she possess that prompted such certainty?

I told you so! Never in all my life have I felt confident enough to say those words and definitely not with an exclamation point. My mother, teachers, psychiatrists, and now the Greek chorus at the Pleasure Palace all provided "help" that did nothing but underscore that I didn't know what the hell I was doing about anything. *Motivate yourself, Jonathan. Life is passing you by. Buckle down. Quit day-dreaming. Think about how to re-channel your emotions, Jonathan. Use your words, not your fists.* And now Shashaunna and her gang telling me on a daily basis that my hair needs cutting, my shoes need soled, my attitude needs dry cleaning. God damn it. They can all go to H E L L, exclamation point!

The woman in the red coat had passed my driveway two days in a row at 5:30 PM, both times unknowingly leaving me messages. It didn't take more than that to set me off. I began to position myself every day I could, 5:30 sharp, behind my bush, notepad in hand, now intentionally hiding.

She didn't let me down. Some days I got home too late and missed her. Those nights were bad. But I made it a priority and soon had a page-full of disconnected words and phrases. In two weeks I developed a list of ten. In a month I had twenty-five. Some were troubling, others soothing, prodding, perplexing. All were intoxicating.

> *Unknowable connections*
>
> *I told you so!*
>
> *Breathe, baby, breathe.*
>
> *You jerk!*
>
> *Forgive me already*
>
> *Ah, the sky*
>
> *Fierce and fascinating*
>
> *Get a grip*
>
> *The mystery of it all*

It was the most satisfying few seconds of each day – the anticipation, the discovery, the payoff, the wonder of what it all meant. I never saw her face. She never knew I was there. The voyeuristic layering was mesmerizing.

I found myself pondering the messages while driving to work, now too deep in thought to be bothered by the mundane maneuverings of my fellow travelers, the red lights now providing a welcomed opportunity for a quick peek at my list.

I began to suspect there was more to these messages than disconnected mumblings. What if a deeper message was waiting to be discovered by connecting the words and phrases; a unified field theory of sorts? Maybe some answer for my own life? Surely our random chance encounter, now scheduled like clockwork, had to be something more than random or chance. I was consumed and I loved it.

Neither my friend Jeremy nor Shashaunna thought much of it, but they didn't dissuade me either. I took that as tacit support.

When I mistakenly called my mother and told her about this most exciting turn of events, she paused, took a deep breath and said that it sounded like I wasn't taking my medication, that I sounded a bit manic. God damn it! Why do I let myself in for her criticism? I knew the truth. It was something bigger than my mother. And I was at the center of it, navigating forces beyond her comprehension. Beyond my comprehension.

Soon, finding out who this woman in the red coat was, where she lived and where she was going each day as she obliviously passed my home became my most cherished desire. I couldn't risk following her and having her see me because it might end our connection. I couldn't bear that. So, I pulled in my friend, Jeremy. He's a lanky red-head a few years older than me and runs his own T-shirt business out of a rented garage down on South Decatur Boulevard, an unlikely entrepreneur and a good friend, non-judgmental and accepting. Plus, he owes me big time for when I drove him all the way to Albuquerque and back during one long four-day weekend to chase after a girl who had broken his heart.

"Just follow her, man. That's all. Find out what you can and report back. But whatever you do, don't talk to her and don't let her see you following her. And for God's sake, if you get discovered, which you better not, don't say anything about me."

It didn't take Jeremy long to develop a dossier on her, as unspectacular as it was. Jeremy called from his cell phone. "OK, here's the scoop. I just heard some lady call out to her, 'Hey, Mary.' She looks about your mother's age. She's stopping in front of the 7/11. Now she's tying up the dog. She's going inside."

After about three such reconnaissance trips, we learned that Mary Henderson lives three blocks away from me and gets home from work at 5:00 PM every weekday and takes her dog out religiously. She walks past my place, down two more blocks, sometimes chatting it up with some other old broads walking their dogs. Then she turns left on Brennan and makes a rectangular route back home. The same route everyday. The dog, Jeremy suspected, was a Portuguese Water Dog. "You know, man, the breed that Obama got 'cause they don't shed and his kids are allergic." I didn't give a damn about the dog, but that's just the kind of minutia that Jeremy always seems to pull out of his back pocket. I guess it helps to know a lot of stuff when you run your own business.

He said she muttered from time to time, but he was never close enough to hear what she said. She always seemed deep in thought and he guessed that sometimes those thoughts just bubbled up like a fart. "It wasn't like she was schizophrenic or anything," he said. "Just lost in thought, man, just lost."

I was sure there was more to it, but I pulled Jeremy off the case and got focused on my new task of breaking the code of those phrases. By now, my refrigerator was covered with blue, yellow and pink Post-Its, each with a verbal gift from the lady in the red coat. I arranged and rearranged them like refrigerator poetry magnets, staring at them all weekend, waiting for my subconscious to detect connections. I guess I was hoping words would light up like they did for Russell Crowe in *A Beautiful Mind,* revealing the deeper meaning. That didn't happen. But I didn't give up.

The next weekend, I pulled out a bottle of Scotch and a package of Old Trapper from The Beef Jerky Store down on 3rd Street. I was in it for the long haul, baby. My mother kept trying to reach me by phone, but I let her go to message. When she started texting me, I turned off my phone so she couldn't chip away at what little self-esteem I had left. I was on a journey and you were either with me or agin me. She obviously didn't get the cosmic possibilities of this encounter.

I started out on Friday night and stayed with it, arranging and rearranging the Post-Its. A few times, I thought I was on to something, like: *Get a grip – you jerk – behold the sky – fierce and fascinating – forgive me everything.* But it didn't quite resonate.

Jeremy stopped in a couple of times and all he said was, "Man, this is starting to freak me out." He took a swig of Scotch, picked up one of the Post-its and tried to reposition it, but I kicked him and he dropped it. Soon, he was no longer there.

To say I lost track of time would be an understatement. Time was no longer part of my reality. Einstein would have been impressed. I didn't realize Monday had come and gone until Jeremy reappeared and said, "Big J, I stopped by your work and you weren't there. Your boss is pissed! What are you doing?" It was Tuesday at 1:00 PM.

"Shit." I was nowhere close to discovering the unified field theory of this mess and I had totally blown off work without calling in or responding to the many phone messages that never made it to my awareness. I jumped up, took off for work in the same clothes I had worn since Friday and walked into the Pleasure Palace reeking.

Martha, my boss, took one look at me and said, "My office, now!" She put me on notice that if I screwed up one more time (*I have a pattern, you see*), I would be out on my ass. Then she sent me home to get cleaned up. As I slunk out of there in a fog, Shashaunna waved me over for what I thought might be some shoring up. "Thanks, you little shit. You totally messed up our production schedule. The catalog didn't get finished and the warehouse is all backed up. We have lives, too. Now we have to work late to make up time."

Two weeks later, I had been toeing the line and was back in their good graces. It was my twenty-ninth birthday, and the Palace gals "surprised" me with the perfunctory breast cake, candles triumphantly planted in two large icing nipples, a bouquet of blown-up colored condoms and entertainment ala the Ladies Gaga (Shashaunna, Martha, Christina and LaVida), bedazzled in neon wigs *(item #472)*, lip-syncing to Beyonce's *Naughty Girl* and waving make-shift microphones from the Glorious Movers and Shakers Vibrator line *(item #696)*, batteries in and operating in their *deeply satisfying, twisting, wiggling and thrusting moves.* It was good-natured and well meant, but it left me feeling empty and sad. I was circling thirty and this was what I had to show for it?

When 5:00 PM came around, everyone headed off to their real life of husbands, boyfriends, dogs and parakeets. I was going home to stand behind my bush and wait for a woman who didn't know I existed. I walked into Martha's office and told her I couldn't do it anymore. I wasn't coming back. Her eyes filled up and she took my hands. "Jonathan, you have so much promise, but what's going to become of you?" I walked out of there holding tight to one of my new-found phrases — *breathe baby, breathe!*

The next two months were a blur. I got lost in several more Scotch and beer binges staring at my metaphysical Post-Its, by then spread across the living room floor, looking for meaning, anything that I could drape my fragile existence around.

My obsession with breaking the code eventually kept me from eavesdropping on the woman in the red coat. *(I'd like to say that I had gotten all that she could give, but I have a history of being caught by something, not able to breathe and then, bam, just like that, I would be done!)* I forgot to pick up my mail, didn't pay my bills and wasn't all that surprised when one night the lights went out, the refrigerator stopped humming and the air conditioner ceased. It was the middle of May and the Vegas temps were starting to hint at what was to come. I opened the windows, drank my Scotch without rocks and lit candles. When the booze ran out, I sat on the floor in a state of nothingness, no longer concerned about cause and effect.

I was immobile. The world turned, the sun appeared, disappeared, appeared again. People materialized through the haze like apparitions. They wanted to pull me out, keep me alive, help me reach the other side of this insanity. Shashaunna, luminescent in the candlelight and smelling of jasmine, offered to give me a bath and cut my hair. I waved her away. Jeremy appeared with his gentle presence, reminding me of the life force waiting for me, when (*if*) I chose to engage. And then, he disappeared. My mother arrived, took one look at me and wailed, her cry reaching down into my core. But it didn't shake me from my spot. She disappeared, like the others and I wondered if they were real or figments of a disturbed mind slipping forever over the edge.

I'd still be sitting there today if it hadn't been for the fire. The candles melted down and caught the Post-Its, turning them into floating wisps like miniature lanterns in the night sky. I watched as my obsession flickered and dissipated into the air, feeling free of it all, of everything. Even when the drapes caught and began to dance, I sat there, sweat dripping down my face.

A fireman got me out. My clothes and hair were singed. The only thing that wasn't destroyed besides me was Buddha. Car, clothes, even the bush I hid behind for months burst into flames. All that was gone except for me and Buddha.

I picked him up, crossed the street and sat cross-legged on the curb, Buddha in my lap, and together we watched the firemen tend to the mess I had created. I felt nothing. Jeremy saw the fire on the local news and came to get us. He took us home, gave us a bath and let us rest for a few days. Then he put us to work. No judgment. No moralizing. He just said that if we were going to live in his apartment, then we were going to help with his business.

Buddha did his job -- he sat. I folded and packed and loaded boxes of T-shirts into the van. Soon, I learned to use the heat transfer press and the six-color heat pressing machine. On the weekends, we set up our booth at Vegas strip mall "art" shows. On First Fridays, we joined other hucksters along Colorado in Downtown Vegas. Our best customers -- the tony Summerlin folk pretending they were street people for a night. Buddha was our mascot. People smiled at him, stopped to look at the T-shirts, chatted us up and eventually pulled out their wallets. Jeremy said Buddha was good for business.

He seemed more concerned than I that my decoding obsession had been destroyed in the fire. I told him the words of the woman in the red coat were emblazoned on my soul. He said that obviously wasn't doing me any good and encouraged me to pick a few good ones and put them on shirts. Shashaunna thought that was a good idea and used her graphic design skills to whip us up a neat logo with a special metaphysical font. We called our line *Buddha Bing*. I picked up a plastic bonsai tree at Pier One, placed it behind Buddha, set out the T-shirts and low and behold – people snapped them up as though they were a fast ticket to nirvana.

Shashaunna kept showing up and encouraging me to get back on meds. She said that if I had a heart condition I wouldn't fight taking a pill to keep me alive. There was something to that, so I let her drive me to my psychiatrist's office.

My obsession had dissipated, or maybe more accurately had ended in destruction, and now I was willing to sit back and let the words earn some bucks and pay me back a bit. Shashaunna wasn't ready to turn the page quite yet. She suspected the words still held a key to some kind of transcendence. She suggested another approach—quit trying to force the words and let them tell their own story.

So, I started taking a pad and pen with me each weekend to the T-shirt booth. I waited for something to take shape. For weeks, nothing. Then I felt a crack in the cement wall of my psyche. A story began to seep out. Soon it flowed. I imagined a woman in a red coat walking her dog, tortured by her own demons, maybe a son that wasn't going to make it, her pleas not enough to save him, her words, unbeknownst to her, slipping into the consciousness of another woman's son, saving him. I wrote about the fierce and fascinating bond of mother and child, one pushing away and the other holding on, both fueled by universal but competing urges.

I wove in the dog and his sense of smell a million times greater than humans. How, with just a sniff, he could discern hundreds of states of grass, friend from foe, fear from frolic, all while we humans clomp Neanderthal-like through the silent world of scent. How the woman and the dog shared time and space but not the same reality. How we are entwined by a thousand unknown connections. And, how the power of words reveals the mystery of these connections and leads to transcendence, if we but sit and wait. The fog was lifting, and soon I had a story.

By the end of summer, I had twelve short stories and called the collection *Oracle in a Red Coat*. By winter, I found a publisher. I had thought about dedicating the book to *Mary Henderson, the woman in the red coat*. I daydreamed about wrapping it up and mailing it to her and her surprise and wonder upon discovering a book dedicated to her, written by someone she had never met. Shashaunna said it might feel awfully creepy for her to discover that she had been stalked and her words stolen. Shashaunna has a good head on her shoulders. My mother might be right, we make a good couple. So, I dedicated it to my mother and *The Little Fat Guy*.

Over beer and pizza at my mom's house, Jeremy, Shashaunna and I talked about this upheaval in my life and what wisdom I might have gained. I don't know that I would call this wisdom, but this ripping open of myself, this welcoming of chaos and the unknown and making peace with it -- I couldn't have done it without them, my bodhisattvas *(Jeremy taught me that word. He keeps surprising me with all the stuff he knows.)*

Snakes

By Hyrum Huskey, Jr.

Ray Larson was thinking about snakes, as he frequently did when driving across the desert barrens of Nevada. He was on his way to a writers' weekend workshop in central California, using the scenic route through Yosemite National Park. Ray had left Las Vegas in early morning darkness with a waning crescent moon still hanging in the sky looking like a lost toenail clipping. Now, three hours later, desert flatland on both sides of Highway 95 was heating up. Ray suspected it was that time of day when rattlesnakes were sunning themselves before retreating underground or to other shady spots as the temperature rose.

He shuddered at the thought, an involuntary response to his life-long fear of snakes. Ray suspected his snake phobia had probably originated in a trauma incident of toddler-hood, but he had never really worked it out to a favorable resolution. Since retiring to Las Vegas, Larson had largely given up hiking in the mountains or rural areas as he had done back in New England.

Sure, there were snakes in the wilder areas back east too, but Ray suspected they were fewer in number and not as hot and bothered as out here in the desert. Besides, Ray had always made it a habit to hike well used foot trails. He always tried to assure snakes knew of his approach by tapping his hiking stick loudly against convenient rocks, giving nearby serpents the opportunity to slither off into the woods and undergrowth.

Maybe it was also age that affected him now. Between possible heat stroke and a predominance of rattlesnakes, the hiking in the hills thing seemed a little riskier for a man in his seventies. Or, maybe that was just the current environmental excuse for his fear of snakes. Certainly, he had no restricting physical limitations that would keep him from shorter hikes in the desert.

Lost in his thoughts on the lonely highway, Ray was startled when he saw a car fifty yards off the road in a small depression and tipped up at a thirty degree angle away from the highway. Simultaneously, he saw the two braking tracks that skipped off the right shoulder. He remembered how he had struggled against sleep himself earlier in the morning. Ray braked quickly and pulled onto the shoulder of the road.

He got out of his pickup. He could not tell for sure if the car was occupied. There were no cars in sight on the highway in either direction. Ray realized he alone was responsible to check whether someone in the car needed help. He took a step toward the desert. Then he froze.

A memory floods Ray's mind. It seems as though a film strip is being projected against his brain at high speed. It is a warm summer day in the country. He is a toddler pushing open a farmhouse screen door to escape from the porch. Coming down the steps he notices a large blacksnake coiled on the root cellar door and takes a step to investigate this new discovery. A scream erupts. A screen door slams. He is snatched up violently by his aunt on a flying run down the sidewalk to the yard gate. Several men are running from the barn. His aunt crushes him to her bosom with one arm and uses the other like a wind vane arrow to dead aim on the snake. His uncle fetches a shotgun. Moments later there is a bang and his aunt jumps backward. Amid a flurry of exclamations the snake is draped over the fence. Ray is hurriedly being carried into the house in his aunt's trembling arms.

A second later the memory was over. Ray knew he must cross the scrubby land stretched out between himself and the crashed car. Someone could still be inside and badly hurt. He scanned the nearby ground in the direction of the car, looking for an open, snake-free path that would hasten his coverage of the distance to the vehicle. Momentarily pushing aside his fears, he took a cautious step forward. He willed himself to hurry but he could feel the soles of his sketchers dragging on the sand as he crept toward the car. He desperately searched the sun-baked surrounding ground. He was sure he heard some pulsating sound, but decided it was only the quickened beat of his own heart. His legs and knees had gone weak for some reason, and for a moment Ray suspected he might faint. He was surprised to find perspiration already spotting his arms. Sweat trickled down in front of his ears.

He tried to make his presence well noticed by repeating "I'm coming to help" in a loud, but quavering, voice. "Perhaps" he thought, "any one of the five kinds of Mohave rattlers out there will just slither off in the opposite direction before I get too close." This reminded him that he should look for the telltale path marking the presence of smaller desert sidewinders. He had read that they moved by sideway thrusts that left a repeated "s" pattern on the ground The ground here, though, was quite hard and Ray was not sure the markings would show.

As Ray approached the car's rear fender he could see a female slumped into an air bag, but he couldn't tell how badly she was hurt. Ray's hopes of having scared off any snakes were dashed a second later. From somewhere beneath the half-tilted car, and much too near his feet, he heard the sound he most wished not to hear: the rapid, whirring buzz of rattles that could only come from a rattlesnake.

Ray's mind went hyper. He could feel his chest expanding and contracting from his now rapid breathing. He knew his legs must be in range of the snake's striking distance. Somewhere he had read that if a rattler doesn't leave of its own accord, the threatened person should slowly back away from the snake, out of its range of smell. Adults didn't usually die of a rattlesnake bite. He himself had once seen a man arriving at a medical clinic in the badlands of South Dakota, who had been bitten four times previous to that day. Hell, he was near the highway and his car. But, what about the woman? If she wasn't dead already, she needed immediate help. He wished he had thought about calling 911 before venturing this far. Cell service, though, was spotty out here, and calling may not have been successful had he tried.

He had to move. Now.

Ray raised his foot a mere half inch and took an almost imperceptible step backward. When he remained unbitten, he took another, and then another. From about ten steps behind the car, he saw a three foot rattlesnake wiggle out from under the automobile, then coil itself mere feet from the driver's front door. Its rattles were vibrating a vigorous warning.

"Damn slithering bastard!" Ray shouted. He wanted to kill that damn snake. His face was flushed with hatred and anger was overriding fear. This snake had delayed him long enough. Ray picked up a nearby small rock and heaved it at the rattler, hoping the snake would find another place to go. The rattlesnake held its ground.

Picking up another rock, Ray decided his next move on impulse. Using a short running start, he heaved himself onto the car's trunk, his chest sprawled over the rear window. Then he scrambled onto the hot roof that was tilted away from the snake's side of the vehicle. He squirmed forward where he hoped to see through the windshield, around the airbag, and further determine the woman's condition.

The driver appeared to be alone and unconscious. Around the side of the windshield, Ray spotted the snake still coiled in a striking position, thrusting its ugly flat head upward in Ray's direction. From the safety of his "high ground," Ray slung his second rock at the snake. For the briefest moment the rattler held its position, but then a car horn, and the yells of several men running toward the wreck, alerted the rattler to the danger of sticking around. It slithered away in retreat between the spotted clumps of sagebrush.

Buoyed by the arrival of help and his own new sense of dominance, Ray slid off the car and opened the unlocked door. The hot roof had left small red patches of burns on his fingers and one palm. The woman appeared to be regaining consciousness. There was an ugly bump on the top of her head and her mouth was bloody from several missing front teeth.

"Is she OK?" a man asked as Ray unfastened the seat belt. It hadn't done much of a job when the car mounted a large boulder and came to a jarring stop.

"I think so" replied Ray, "looks like she hit the car roof."

"Did either of you call 911?"

"Yeah, I did" said the second new arrival. "An ambulance is coming." A distant siren confirmed his assertion.

Ray and the others helped the injured woman down from her car and sat her on a sweater that had been in the front passenger seat of the car. Then Ray went to his pickup for water and a light blanket that he carried along with a small first aid kit. He moved more quickly on the return trip but was still careful to look well ahead on his path. After all, he figured, the rattlesnake he had encountered was likely not the only one around. He had no desire to be the man God had suggested in the Bible would crush a serpent under his heel.

Ray had the woman lie down on the blanket and gave her a sip of water to drink. He elevated her feet on a flat rock.

A few minutes later, a policeman and two ambulance attendants marched over from the highway in unison. Signage on the vehicles indicated they had come from nearby Beatty where Ray had eaten breakfast a short time earlier in a casino. The patrolman took a report on Ray's actions, seemingly unconcerned about the snake encounter, and then gathered the personal identifying data of everyone involved. The woman admitted falling asleep.

Two days later, on the final night of his workshop, Ray had a dream. It was identical to one he had also dreamed twenty years earlier, and totally unlike the snake dreams he occasionally had where snakes were always menacing or slithering in heaps around him. At the time of the earlier dream, Ray was seeing a counselor and wrestling with some religious issues.

Ray is at some sort of garden party when a huge snake arrives. The snake is strangely not scary, because it is dressed out as a clown with vivid red, green, and yellow patches. The snake is wearing a large ribbon below its head and prancing about while standing on the tip of its tail end. The snake has a dopey looking face and everything about its appearance seems designed to dismiss any negative emotions and yet draw attention to itself.

In the earlier instance of this dream, the counselor had told him the snake represented a universal religious symbol and Ray's religious struggle at the time, and was designed to draw Ray's attention in a way to help him make the decision to leave his religion behind. Re-dreaming the dream now, the clownish snake seemed to be a sign that Ray's snake phobia was exaggerated and unduly hindering his enjoyment of the outdoors. The snake's dancing celebrated Ray's partial overcoming of fear to successfully help the accident victim. At least that was the way Ray chose to interpret the dream at this point in his life.

At breakfast the following morning, before starting his trip home, Ray struck up a conversation with another attendee at the workshop. Over coffee, the conversation turned to the incident with the snake on route to the workshop. Ray confessed that he had always been afraid of snakes in general and, except for viewing them in captivity, had only a few actual encounters with them in his lifetime.

"It's strange" he told his breakfast companion, "I was even able to deal with a snake like that this late in life."

"Emergency. Brings out our best traits" said his companion, "Your concern for the person in the wreck must have let you set aside your fear, at least long enough to help."

"You think it will carry over?" Ray asked.

"Perhaps, who knows?"

After breakfast, Ray Larson began his trip home. Along the way he stopped at a toy shop to purchase something for his two young granddaughters who also lived in Las Vegas. The toy shop's inventory included two plush green snakes with silly looking faces that made Ray laugh when he spotted them. He purchased the stuffed snakes and flung them loosely coiled on the passenger seat, where they--and he--rode comfortably together all the way home.

And that is why, arriving safely in his upscale neighborhood, Randy was so startled to see a rattlesnake sunning itself at the corner of his garage door.

The End

The Flight of the Eagle Feather

By Noëlle de Beaufort

The Paiute Brave
Sierra Nevada Mountains
March 1825

A watcher would think the still woman a statue, carved in granite. The Paiute brave crouched behind a dense pine grove, watching the tribe's shaman, Red Sunset, in the small clearing. The gift of future vision, bestowed upon her by the Great Spirit, shattered ancestral traditions. She had succeeded her long-dead twin brother as shaman. Tonight, she sat in the midst of a ceremonial circle of stones, her chanting virtually inaudible.

The luminescent moon glowed in the brilliant blackness of the night. A shooting star arced overhead. *A sign. What has she seen?*

She stood, facing away from him and stepped over the stones, raising her hands to the sparkling stationary stars and their moving portent.

"Fear not, my son."

How did she know he was there? It had always been so. He could not hide from her special sight.

"Curiosity, Mother, not fear. What did you see?"

She turned toward him. "Before two winters, he will return."

She speaks of the stranger. The stranger who had fulfilled his uncle's quest and saved the Snow Tribe was a tale he knew well. The uncle and the stranger both loomed in his imagination, like ghosts as mysterious as that shooting star.

*****

Jean-Louis
Ravenshire Farms, New York
March 1825

Something is wrong. The mare's gait has slowed. She is afraid to jump. "Sacré bleu!" Jean-Louis Chevalier pulled his boots out of the stirrups just as his horse skidded to an abrupt stop. His experienced muscles reacted instinctively, propelling him over the three-foot-high stone wall. After landing on the soft grass, he rolled sideways to a stop.

Riders who had jumped earlier were galloping toward the next hurdle. Jumpers trailing him might land too close. Dimly sensing the danger, he tried to stand, but his left leg failed him and he fell back to the ground. Drifting in and out of consciousness, he heard someone calling his name.

*****

Jean-Louis detected conversation around him before he could open his eyes or speak.

"Your man is coming around," said the young physician.

Gabriella Windward James, known as Bri, shook her head in disagreement. "He is not 'my man.' Jean-Louis is a loyal retainer and friend who saved my life on more than one occasion."

Jean-Louis grimaced in pain. His body felt as if it had been driven over by a runaway stagecoach. The physician poked at his leg, applying pressure. He tried to lift his head, groaning. One eye opened.

"Ah ha!" The doctor put his finger on his patient's neck. "Pulse is returning to normal. A man your age shouldn't be jumping horses over stone fences."

Jean-Louis stared at him with disdain. "You are a young fool."

Taken aback, the doctor sputtered. " Your comment is inappropriate, sir."

"As was yours. What have you done to me?"

"I have set your broken leg. As you were unconscious, you felt no pain. You should heal in time."

"How much time?"

"For a man your age-"

Jean-Louis glared. "Guard your tongue, young fool."

Bri gestured to the doctor to leave the room. She leaned over the patient. "Jean-Louis, I feared we'd lost you."

He shrugged his shoulders. "Now we know the mare's not a jumper."

"Fine way to discover that!" Bri scowled at him. "I can't tell Uncle Henry that you died jumping an untried horse."

"He'd laugh. It would be ironic for me to die that way. I already know where I will die, and it's not here."

"You hit your head when you fell. No one knows the place of one's death."

"I do." He smiled.

"Inscrutable as ever." Edward, Bri's husband, walked into the room and hugged her. "Dr. McCullough is in a bit of a huff, darling. That must mean our patient is awake." He turned to Jean-Louis. "Bri wanted to ride that new horse. You probably saved her neck. Again."

Bri touched her protector's arm. "I'm going to ask Mrs. Jackson to bring you some chicken and celery soup."

Jean-Louis nodded and closed his eyes. *Perhaps it is time to go. I might not be so lucky next time.*

*****

Ohio River Valley
March 1826

During the long trip from New York on a ship moving through the newly opened Erie Canal through Lake Erie to Ohio, trekking overland to the Ohio River, crossing the Mississippi River, then riding west towards Independence, Missouri, Jean-Louis reflected on the course of his life. Of many adventures, two stood out: meeting Red Buffalo in the western Canadian prairies in 1784 and encountering Henry Windward, then a Viscount, son of the 10th earl of Ravenshire, in Northern Canada in 1792.

*****

Henry had been on a trading mission to the Hudson's Bay Company to negotiate the importation of beaver, otter, marten, mink and fox fur to European markets.

Impressed that the son of a British earl had built a worldwide trading company at the young age of thirty-two, the company's managing director, Pierre Stellaire, invited Henry to go on a hunt in the northern near-wilderness.

Intrigued, Henry agreed. They traveled up the St. Lawrence River to their remote destination.

Accompanied by Pierre and his intrepid Métis Indian guide, Michif, the group's first day frustrated their expectations. Freezing sleet blasted their faces as they raced over the starkly beautiful arctic tundra. As twilight fell, their swift dogsleds sped into the local trading post surrounded by fully outfitted cabins as well as bunkhouses for the trappers and guides.

Henry and Pierre trudged into the saloon and commandeered a corner table and ordered whiskey. Suddenly, the double doors opened and a fierce wind blew in a snow-covered trapper.

A French-accented voice boomed. "After a day like this, the fires of hell will be welcome!"

Fast on the French trapper's heels was Michif. He threw his arm over the Frenchman's shoulder and said, "No luck, eh, Jean-Louis?"

"*Au contraire, mon ami.* Today I threw a spear into the heart of a polar bear!"

The saloon patrons convulsed in laughter. "Jean-Louis, your lies are legendary," said the barkeep. "Did you bag an arctic hare, put it in a fox skin and expect us to mistake it for a polar bear?" The yelps and jeers continued until the Métis held up his hands to stop the chatter.

"This man is the best trapper on the continent. If he says he bagged a polar bear, then he did."

"They never come this far south," argued another guide. "I've heard this fairy tale before: the beast was too large to transport and is in a location only you know."

"*C'est vrai.*" Jean-Louis looked around the room until he had everyone's attention. He spotted the Hudson's Bay man. "Monsieur Stellaire, I invite you and your friend to come with me tomorrow to confirm the kill. I need more dogs and a larger sled to skin my prize and bring the spoils back here."

Henry stood, raised his glass and said, "We accept. Come join us."

The Métis escorted Jean-Louis to the table. The French trapper entertained them with stories until the dawn was near breaking.

Jean-Louis saw the skepticism in the Viscount's eyes, but also a measure of respect between men who recognize another intrepid explorer. He knew then that the English Viscount would play a role in his life.

After a few hours sleep, Michif and Jean-Louis secured the appropriate gear and headed north with Pierre and Henry. Pristine jagged peaks were partially obscured by an iridescent haze swirling among the summits. Approaching a frozen lake bed, they spotted a broken section of ice and heard a plaintive bleating sound.

"What is that?"

"More bears. Take care." The Métis reached for his pistol, kept warm inside his fur covering.

In the terrain of fluffy cream, mounds of snow flung indiscriminately by the fierce cold winds, Henry narrowed his eyes. "By God, Jean-Louis, I believe you have done it!"

Their snowshoes helped them glide over the snowfall as they made their way over to the mound, which Jean-Louis had used to disguise the carcass from hungry wild predators. Michif brushed off wisps of snow. His actions uncovered an ear. Soon, a pair of haunting black eyes stared into the cloudy sky. More of the magnificent animal emerged until the full carcass of a large male polar bear was revealed.

"Is the sled big enough?" Pierre rubbed his chin in doubt. "What about other bears? Maybe a pack is nearby." His scanned the landscape with a furtive glance.

"Male polar bears are solitary hunters. We are not taking the carcass. Only the skin, claws and teeth are transportable. The beast weighs over a ton."

Henry was puzzled. "What about the flesh?"

"Worms permeate their flesh and cause disease; the

liver poisons dogs. Lesson for you, Viscount: Men don't eat polar bears."

The strange sounds began again. Jean-Louis turned slowly toward the break in the lake ice. A small head bobbed up. Then another. Then a larger one. "A mother and her cubs. No sudden movements. If she charges, shoot her."

Henry disagreed. "Then the cubs will die."

Jean-Louis nodded."If I hadn't killed the male, he would have killed them anyway. It's the way of the north."

The Viscount was persistent. "Can we distract them while we skin the male? Perhaps the dogs will frighten them long enough for us to get away."

"*C'est possible*. But we must be prepared for unexpected actions."

The Métis brought the sled and dogs to the carcass; he and Jean-Louis set to its skinning while Henry and Pierre kept watch. Michif then hacked out its teeth while Jean-Louis cut out its claws. It took the strength of the quartet to lift the skin onto the sled, and Jean-Louis lashed it to the carrier with leather straps.

Jean-Louis prepared to steer the sled with the silvery skin. Jean-Louis petted the lead dog. "I've never driven a team this large."

"No one has, Frenchman." The Métis took one last

look at the polar bear and her cubs. "You are a hunter...you will save your children. May the Great Spirit protect you."

"There you go, making me a villain again." Jean-Louis waved the reins and the sled began to move. "Hunters hunt. This bear will be a great rug for some stuffy old English nobleman. Any ideas on who might buy it?" He winked at Henry.

The dogs moved forward, straining under the weight of the skin.

*****

After the hunt, Jean-Louis had accompanied Henry back to London. Bri had been just a toddler then. He'd given her that nickname because Lady Gabriella seemed too formal for the headstrong child. For more than thirty years, in his role as bodyguard, driver and friend, the Windward family had been the focus of his life. Now he would reclaim his destiny.

*****

Independence, Missouri
April 1826

Jean-Louis rode into Independence, pelted by a hard rain and eager for shelter. His instincts about the horse he had spotted in Ohio and bought for a pittance had been correct. A gentle touch, a calm tone, and a seasoned hand on the reins tamed the unruly animal. The black-and-white speckled gelding could run like an Arabian, but demonstrated the endurance of a prairie workhorse. Trailed by a mule packed with dried food, water, bedroll and other supplies, he marveled at how this sleepy outpost had been transformed into a boomtown when the first mule trains had formed there a few months earlier.

The network of French fur trappers and traders passed on information to their compatriots . The non-French were occasionally led astray or misdirected to hostile territory if they disdained the trappers. Jean-Louis spotted a stable with a French name and rode up to the entry of Robineau Trading and Stables, a large area with water troughs and posts to tie up horses and mules.

A scrawny teenage stable boy waved him into the main barn to get out of the rain.

He dismounted, shook the water off his hat and poncho. "*Merci*."

"Mercy yourself, sir. I don't speak much Frenchy. My pa does, but he told me to learn the native tongues, so I speak English and some Indian dialects." He gestured toward an office. "Pa's in there."

"Thanks." He trudged over the muddied wooden planks and knocked on the doorjamb. "What's the cost for a night's boarding for a horse and mule?"

Robineau looked up and said, "*Bienvenue*! A Frenchman speaking British-accented English. Canada?"

"Aix originally, then Canada, London and New York. Bound for the Sierra Nevada. Know of any mule trains that need drivers?" Jean-Louis had a pension from Henry, who was now earl, but he thrived on work. He believed that leisure made men lazy and he knew the western wilderness was no place for a lazy man.

Robineau nodded. "Try Big Jim Campbell. He runs the Black Elk saloon. All the mule train leaders go there, and they have clean and decent rooms."

"*Merci.*"

"*De rien, mon frère.*"

Big Jim Campbell was innkeeper, barkeep and informal mayor of the mule train drivers. He was not tall, but got his nickname from his rotund physique. His ruddy face was framed by an unruly shock of black hair tinged with white, and was clearly in charge, shouting curses at anyone who didn't behave well, which seemed to Jean-Louis to be most of the rough-edged clientele.

Jean-Louis walked up to the bar, asked for a whiskey, and told Big Jim that Robineau had sent him.

Big Jim slammed the whiskey down with a flourish. "Driver or drover?"

"Driver. Heading to the Sierra Nevada."

The proprietor tilted his head toward a man at a table at the back of the saloon. "Capt. Jasper's leaving soon for the Utah Nevada Territory – hell of a wild area, that."

Jean-Louis nodded. "Many years ago, I traded with the Paiute."

"Captain Jasper is one of the few who knows how to get to the northwest without dying of thirst or arrows. Some tribes want to be paid for passage or trade for guns; others just don't want you in their territory at all. The wife will give you a room key and show you where things are. We've even got a Chinaman who does the laundry."

Jean-Louis shrugged and smiled. "You noticed."

A weather beaten cowboy caught Big Jim's eye. "Hey, Joe, you mangy dog! Get your goddamned feet off the table!" He waved Jean-Louis toward the captain.

The captain looked up. "Driver or drover?"

"Driver. Looking to get to the Sierra Nevada."

"In two days. Background?"

After Jean-Louis explained his trapping and driving experience, the captain smiled. "So you've driven dogs and horses, but only trailed mules behind a horse. Still, it's all about the same. Pay's decent, more if you're a good shot."

"I am."

The captain's eyes told Jean-Louis that no further explanation was necessary. "Why do they call you captain?"

"Army. War of 1812. Liked the west. Stayed."

"It's addictive, I agree." Waving his hands as he spoke, Jean-Louis continued, "Vast prairies, stark deserts, imposing mountains, plunging canyons, raging rivers, pristine lakes. The city is like a prison compared to the wild, open, ever-changing western frontier."

The captain laughed. "Maybe you should write penny novels. You have a poetic way of talking."

"Freedom releases the poetry of a man's soul."

"Are you a drinking man?"

"When I was young, trapping in northern Canada, I learned quickly that alcohol dulls a man's senses and leaves him vulnerable to the dangers of the unknown. One a day is my limit now."

"Good. Drunks are unreliable. Sometimes I have no choice; I may need you to help me rein in the undisciplined."

"As you wish."

*****

Following the trail to the west, mules, cows, sheep and assorted cargo were traded along the route. The journey was dusty and exhausting, but not uneventful. An ambush by vagrants looking for an easy score was rebuffed by the sharply honed shooting skills of the captain and Jean-Louis, but a Comanche attack left him with a shoulder wound from an arrow. Lucky for the mule train, the band of young stragglers was no match for the seasoned captain and Jean-Louis. Months after his fifteen-hundred-mile trek, Jean-Louis bade the captain, "*Adieu*", and branched off toward his destination.

****

Utah Nevada Territory
September 1826

As he crossed the high desert plateau, Jean-Louis saw his destination come closer each day. This night, the distinctive Sierra Nevada peaks of the Snow Tribe of the Paiutes rose in the twilight, clouds bathed in hues of magenta and violet.

He fed his horse and mule, and tied them to a stake in the ground. The terrain had changed from prairie to forest, providing fuel for a longer-lasting fire than scraggly bushes over the months. Earlier in the day, he'd spotted a desert hare. Pierced expertly by his arrow, it roasted as night fell. The sky darkened under a pearlescent moon surrounded by an explosion of stars. *Londoners rarely see the stars. No wonder they scatter about like moths seeking light.* The nights were colder now, and the snow on the mountains edged farther down. *With luck, I will arrive before the snows start.*

As was his custom, Jean-Louis wrote in his diary each evening, sketching out any interesting landmarks or game, and appending brief thoughts on the day, impressions of people he'd met, and reflections on life. He had left the earlier volumes of his adventures with Bri in New York, instructing her to do with them as she wished. By now, he knew, she would have read far enough in his worn leather tomes to understand why he had left. Perhaps someday she would receive his final thoughts, dreams and tales.

Although his leg had healed, a dull ache remained. The shoulder wound from the arrow loosed in the Comanche attack in Colorado had also healed, but occasional thrusting pain when he twisted or moved could momentarily paralyze him. At least it was his left shoulder, although he had taught himself to use either hand in knife-throwing, shooting, and punching. It was a critical skill in this unpredictable wilderness.

He dreamed of his love, Red Sunset, female shaman of the Snow Tribe. Many years earlier, he had fulfilled the quest undertaken by her brother, Red Buffalo, who had died in his arms. Jean-Louis had delivered the herbs Red Buffalo had found, and saved the tribe. Red Sunset dreamed during their brief interlude that they would die together. Her trances were visions into the truth; his faith in destiny had never wavered. *She still lives.*

*****

He reached the mountain in early October. The trail was arduous, but the markers were as he remembered. He was winded from the climb, leading the horse and mule, chilled by the early frost that covered the ground. Light was waning. *Is this the cave? Have I found it at last?*

He pulled the tired animals into the shelter, tied them to a stake he pounded into the earth, and stood to survey the scene. In the darkness, he walked to the edge and ran his hand along the wall. *Yes!* His initials were where he had carved them over forty years earlier.

"We are almost there," he said to the animals. He fed them, then made a small fire by the opening of the cave, skinned and roasted two doves for dinner.

He fell asleep to the rhythm of the breaths of his companions, warmed by the fire. He was awakened by the crack of a twig outside the cave in the predawn hour. He did not move, opening one eye to assess the danger. The horse and mule still slept silently. *Why are they calm?* It took a few moments for his eye to adjust to the darkness. Three figures of white fur sat outside the cave. *Bears?* He did not recall seeing white bears away from the far northern coast. *Silver foxes? Too large. Snow wolves? Too small.* He squinted. *A black braid against the white fur. Paiutes. Did Red Sunset dream I was here?*

He opened the other eye and focused. Dawning light shone on the white fur like an aura. I have come so far. *If they meant me harm, my throat would have been slit as I slept.*

He sat up and stared back at them. The dawn's beams appeared like icicles dripping over his watchers.

"*Shan-loo-ee.* At last."

Her voice silenced his.

She rose and walked toward him, the red of her hair now streaked with white, the green eyes clear as ever, touching his soul.

He stood and held out his arms to her.

She embraced him. "I dreamed of you. Now meet my husband, the chief of the Snow Tribe."

Husband? Cursed Fate! Is my dream lost forever?

The man approached. Older than Jean-Louis, the chief was still spry, white-haired and exuded a command presence. "*Shan-loo-ee.* Welcome. I remember you."

"You speak well."

"We trade with white man. Learn his language."

Jean-Louis scanned the man's features. "You were the younger brave who tracked me to the cave that day so long ago."

The chief nodded. "*Hainch K-tum-ar-g.*"

"I remember, 'Friend, talk it out', as Red Buffalo taught me. Who is the brave behind you? Your son?" Anguish clouded his face. *I have missed so much.*

"We have two children. I accepted this one as son. His name is *Bagootsoo Fran-say.* Your son."

Red Sunset motioned to French Buffalo to come forward. "I named him for you and my brother."

Nearly forty, *Bagootsoo Fran-say's* blue eyes and wavy light brown hair set him apart from his tribe. Sinewy and shorter than the chief, he was the same height as Jean-Louis.

"Mother always said you would return someday. For long time, anger lived in my heart. Father, the chief, taught me anger is weakness. It is gone now. Mean you to stay?"

Jean-Louis nodded. Tears spilled from his eyes. He held out his arms to embrace his son. "I'm sorry I left, sorry you were angry. I didn't know about you. Please forgive me."

"The past is over. You are here and I welcome you. The Snow Tribe awaits you with a feast."

Jean-Louis smothered the fire, gathered his animals, and followed his greeters along the rocky trail toward the village camp of the Snow Tribe. He led his horse while French Buffalo led the mule. Suddenly, the horse neighed and began to rear and the mule stubbornly stopped, refusing to move. Jean-Louis felt the hairs on his neck rise. *A predator.*

The growl was low, menacing and came from above them. Moving only his eyes upward, Jean-Louis saw a cougar on the rocks above. "Do not move," he said. "Arrows are not enough. If he jumps, we cannot hit true. A knife in the neck is the best. Move ahead, slowly." He moved his left hand behind him to retrieve his knife when the pain of his shoulder radiated down to his hand, causing him to gasp, spurring the cougar to action. It leapt toward him as he raised his knife to inflict a fatal wound. He didn't see the movement that knocked him to the ground, sheltering him. The chief had his knife out and thrashed at the cougar, but the big cat's jaws closed on his arm and ripped into him, dragging the wounded chief a few yards away. Jean-Louis sprang to his feet and stabbed the cat repeatedly. French Buffalo joined him and together they killed the killer.

The chief spurted blood from his mouth.

Red Sunset ran to him. "No! You must not die!"

"It is my time, my love. This you know. This you have dreamed. Our life together ends. Your new life begins. I go happily to the Great Spirit. Son, be a just chief. Trust your instincts."

Jean-Louis said, "If we get you back to the village, Red Sunset can heal you."

The chief smiled at Jean-Louis through blood-stained teeth. "No, my friend. It is done. I am at peace and so be you all." At that moment, an eagle feather floated down and landed on his chest.

"The Great Spirit has blessed you, Father. *Kasa,* the sacred feather of an eagle, has flown to carry you to the Great Spirit in the sky."

The chief's last act was to look at Red Sunset. When his eyes stared into nothingness, she gently closed them and began a soft chant.

Jean-Louis and French Buffalo draped the chief's body over the horse, and tied the cougar to the mule. At the village, a funeral pyre was prepared for the chief. Chanting lasted until the ashes were cold. The cougar was roasted for the tribe to consume; the chief consumed the heart of the wild cat in tribal ritual.

As French Buffalo donned the headdress of chief, Jean-Louis looked up. An eagle flew high, disappearing into the clouds shrouding the peak of the sacred mountain of the Snow Tribe.

Walking the Bristlecone Trail

By Ernest Walwyn

"Better be life or death or I'll kill whoever that is," Kevin mumbled. His brow creased and his lips formed a thin line. He had just settled down in front of the TV to watch a baseball game when a frantic banging on the door coupled with a constant ringing of the doorbell disturbed him. He opened the door to see Eric shaking, his eyes wide with fright.

"Eric, what's wrong?"

"It's Paige. She went walking this morning on the Bristlecone Trail. She's usually home by noon or shortly after. It's already two. I think she might be in trouble. Can you please help?"

"Of course. What can I do?" His annoyance turned to worry for his friend.

"I don't have a way to get up there. Would you drive me and help me look for her?" He stood just inside the doorway, wringing his hands.

"Of course. Let me get my keys. I'll bring some rope just in case."

"Thank you. Thank you. I came to you because of your climbing experience. I hope you don't have to use it." Eric grabbed Kevin by the shoulders and hugged him.

Kevin gathered rope and other items he thought they would need. They headed out the door.

In the car they headed north out of Las Vegas on the I-95. Once past the city limits the traffic thinned out enough so that he could drive well over the speed limit. On the way, Eric told Kevin, "I've walked the trail with her before. Because of my problem with heights I can only go so far on the trail."

"I didn't know you had that fear."

"Yeah. I found out when we took a trip to the Grand Canyon with her sister. It got so bad I couldn't move and could hardly breathe."

"I take it this mountain doesn't affect you as bad as the Canyon did."

"No. Like I said, I can walk part of it. Oh, yeah. After about 4000 feet there's no cell phone service."

"That could be a problem up there."

Eric nodded.

Traffic was light going in their direction on the Lee Canyon road.

Kevin had never been on this road before and marveled at the Joshua trees and Yucca plants that looked like they had been planted in an organized orchard.

It took less than forty-five minutes to reach the Lower Bristlecone Trailhead. The whole trip normally took an hour.

In the parking lot, they found Paige's car. Eric put his hand on the hood. He looked at Kevin. "It's cold."

Kevin nodded. "That means she's been gone for a while. Let's go."

The two men started the uphill hike looking for signs of Paige along the way. They called her name every so often. "From here it usually takes about three hours to reach the end. Or so Paige tells me. I haven't been able to get to the end."

After a half hour, Eric's breathing started to become labored. It wasn't long before he was panting.

Kevin stopped and waited while Eric caught his breath. "Eric?"

"I'll be okay in a few seconds. Going uphill from eight thousand feet when you're not in shape and worried, it takes its toll."

When he was breathing almost normally again, they continued their climb. In most places the path was covered with loose stones, the treacherous path made it easy to twist an ankle if care weren't taken.

The trail wound around the side of the mountain. This allowed the right side to rise sharply while the left side appeared to drop off steeply, making the trees in the distance appear to be floating. Eric's breathing became more erratic. "I can't. I can't."

"Do you want to stay here and wait?"

"No," he said, shaking his head. "We've got to find Paige."

As the two men trudged along, it seemed to Eric that the trees nearest them passed quickly while those in the distance moved more slowly. Eric's brain was unable to focus on both sets of trees at the same time and switched back and forth between them. His left eye would focus on the near trees while his right focused on those farther away. The changes caused him to stagger. His head began to spin.

"Eric!" Kevin shouted and ran to his friend.

Eric was down on his right knee supporting himself with his right hand. His left hand was waving as if warding off . . . something.

"Eric. What's wrong?"

"Dizzy. Can't catch my breath. Can't focus." He shook his head as he tried to look at Kevin. Now on both hands and knees, he was gasping for breath.

"Son of a . . . Eric. What's wrong?"

In between gasps, he said, "Problem with drop-offs. Get dizzy. Can't breathe. Need a little time."

Kevin knelt beside him. "What can I do?"

Eric lifted his left hand. "Help me up. Got to find Paige," he gasped.

"You sure you can go on?"

"Have to. Have to," he panted.

Kevin helped him up, his arm around his friend's shoulder. They continued up the hill, calling out Paige's name every so often.

They moved slowly at first, then as Eric seemed to get stronger, they were able to quicken their pace.

After five minutes Eric stopped and shouted, "NO!" He covered his face with his hands.

"Eric?"

Almost crying, his hands still covering his face, he said, "Wants me to look. Can't walk and look. Can't."

"What are you talking about? Who wants you to look? What are you supposed to look at?"

"The trees. Wants me to look at the trees."

"Who does? Who wants you to look at the trees? What makes you want to do this?"

"The mountain. Knows if I look I'll go that way, toward the ledge, toward the other trees." He shook his head as if to clear it. "I'll fall if I do that. I'll die and not find her."

Kevin looked to his left. The scenery was more than beautiful; it was magnificent. There was still snow on the peaks, resembling a chocolate cake with melted vanilla icing dribbling down the sides. He said, "Wow, Eric. This is really fantastic. Especially with no cars, no planes, no people. I never knew all this existed so close to where I live."

Eric stood with one hand over his eyes, the other resting on his knee as he bent over, breathing heavily.

"Shit! Sorry. I got carried away by the view." He moved to Eric and took him by the arm. "Ready?"

Eric straightened up and nodded. His eyes were still closed. He opened them slowly focusing on his right. He nodded again and they continued up the hill.

Kevin took occasional peeks to his left and noticed a breeze made the branches wave. *Are they trying to get our attention or saying "Hello"?* He shook the thought from his head and concentrated on Eric.

"How far up does the trail go?"

"About three and a half miles, then there's a sharp rise we have to climb. On the other side the trail gets narrow."

Because of the loose gravel, the uphill climb and Eric's problem it took another hour to reach the point Eric had mentioned.

They stopped and looked at the rise. Although both were six feet tall, neither could see over the top.

Kevin said, "You want me to go first?"

Eric nodded. "Please."

Kevin had to use his hands and feet to get over the rise. He didn't realize Eric was following so close behind him. On the other side, Kevin slid down to the bottom of the rise. Eric almost tumbled into him as he came down.

Kevin looked ahead at the continuation of the trail. Previously, it had been wide enough for two cars to pass side-by-side. Now it was barely wide enough for two people to walk abreast. He turned to look at Eric.

Eric sat on the trail with his eyes closed and his legs pulled up under his chin. His arms were wrapped around his legs.

"Eric, we have to find her."

Eric nodded and held out his hand.

Kevin pulled Eric to his feet.

With his eyes still closed, Eric said, "The only way I can do this is to focus on your feet. If I look at anything else I won't be able to move." As he spoke his eyes started darting left and right. His breath came in short bursts. "It's already started. The trail is getting narrower, the drop-off steeper. Soon there won't be enough room to stand, much less walk.

Let's go. Let's go while I can still move."

Kevin turned and slowly started ahead. He moved a little faster when he felt Eric's hand on his shoulder.

Still moving slowly, they called Paige's name, waited a few seconds, then called again.

When they had walked for twenty minutes, they called and thought they heard her answer.

Up ahead, Kevin saw a place where the trail had collapsed. When they reached the spot, he told Eric to sit.

Kevin looked over the edge and saw Paige about thirty feet down. She stood with one foot on a tree root and one hand holding a branch.

It's a good thing I brought the rope. Otherwise she's too far down to reach. "Eric, we've found her. We'll have to bring her up with the rope. I'll need your help."

He turned back to Paige. "If I lower the rope to you, can you tie it around your waist so we can pull you up?"

"No," she said weakly. "I think I broke my arm."

He turned back to Eric. "One of us has to go down to her."

Eric took a deep breath, looked up at Kevin and said, "Okay. I'll go."

"You sure?"

He nodded. "She's my wife. I have to save her."

Kevin looked at him for a few seconds, then said, "Okay. Let me find a tree to anchor the rope to."

After Eric tied the rope to a nearby tree on the other side of the trail then made a harness and tied it around Eric with a slipknot.

Eric, with his eyes closed, slipped over the side. Once his head was down past the level of the trail, he opened his eyes so he could see how he was going to help Paige. He made sure he kept his focus directly ahead or up to Kevin.

When he was level with her he called to Kevin to stop lowering him. As much as he could, he checked her over. Her left arm was hanging by her side and her blouse was stained with dirt from sliding down the mountain. He could see a tear in the leg of her jeans.

"Can you move?" he asked Paige.

"I'm afraid to try." Her voice was just above a whisper.

He dug one of his toes into the soft soil of the mountain. He stood on the root with Paige with the other. He used one hand to hold onto a branch while he undid the harness. Holding on to the rope he managed to tie it around her chest and under her arms. Because she was so close to the mountain it took more time than he thought it would.

Because it was taking so long, Kevin called down, "Eric, is everything going okay?"

"Yes. Just need a few more seconds." When she was secure, Eric put his arms under hers to hold onto the rope. He called to Kevin, "Okay, we're ready."

Kevin started pulling them up.

Paige used her feet to assist him and held onto the rope with her good arm.

Suddenly, they dropped about ten feet.

Paige screamed.

Panic blanked Eric's mind.

They stopped abruptly and bounced several times.

"What happened?" Eric called when he could breathe again.

"The tree came loose."

When Eric looked up he could see the top of the tree edging slowly past Kevin's head.

"I can't hold you," Kevin called. "The tree is pushing me over. Too much weight."

Eric kissed Paige on the back of her neck and whispered, "I love you." He let go.

"Eric!" Paige screamed as she felt his weight leave her. She put her head against her arm and cried. She didn't realize

Kevin had managed to pull her up until she felt his hands on her arm.

As he pulled her onto the trail, she could see the tree he had used for an anchor. It completely covered the trail. They would have to climb through the branches.

Kevin held her as she sobbed uncontrollably.

"He let go. He let go," she cried.

"Your combined weight was pulling me and the tree over the edge. He gave himself up for us."

Because of the heavy brush and steepness of the hillside, it took three days to find Eric's body. Paige and Kevin were with the rescuers every day until the body was recovered. As they loaded him into the ambulance, one of the men said, "It looks like he's smiling."

Kevin nodded. "He knows his wife is safe, thanks to him."

The rescuer started to say something, then thought better of it and said, "How can he . . . Oh. I see," he said.

Eric was buried several days later. Those whose lives he had touched attended the funeral. On his headstone, after his name and dates of birth and demise were the words he had wanted inscribed. "He cared."

Granddaddy's Gun

By Richard J. Warren

The model 1861 Navy Colt revolver held a special place on the mantel above the fireplace. The blue-plum patina barrel gleamed and the oak handle grips were well-oiled and in superb condition. Meticulously maintained and in perfect working order, this rare specimen was worth thousands of dollars – but it was not for sale. It was priceless. It was Granddaddy's gun.

Luke sat up in bed and saw a flash of bare skin move across the bathroom doorway. The sound of the hair dryer told him it was time to get up and start his day. He padded his way to the kitchen wearing only his boxers and found, as expected, that coffee was waiting in the pot. Cup in hand, he settled down at the kitchen table and opened yesterday's newspaper. Twenty minutes later he heard her coming his way. She entered the kitchen dressed for work wearing a beige pantsuit with a white silk blouse and carrying her heels.

"Hey sleeping beauty," she said as she poured coffee into her to-go mug.

"Hey gorgeous."

She came toward the table, cup in hand. A curious and concerned look came over her face as she touched the purplish bruise on his chest.

"That looks like it hurts, how'd you do that?"

"Rough sex – you bit me last night, remember?"

"Did I?" She bit her lower lip as she giggled. "I guess I got carried away, I'm sorry."

"I'll forgive you – but only if you promise to do it again."

She was at the counter adding cream and putting the lid on her cup when he came up behind her and softly kissed her neck as his right hand went around her waist and cupped her left breast.

"Mmmm, I love you too, but I need my boob back so I can go to work."

He let go and backed away. "Okay, but your ass is mine when you get home."

She laughed. "Oh no, it's my ass – but feel free to kiss it."

"Very funny, how you get to be so hilarious?"

"It's a special talent. Don't forget, we have to meet with the photographer tonight."

"Tonight?"

"Yes Romeo, tonight. The wedding is less than three weeks away, unless you're getting cold feet."

"Not a chance."

"The hall needs the rest their money too."

"Don't worry, it's covered."

Luke watched her walk out the door as he wondered how he got so lucky. Their meeting was pure chance. It was at a friend's wedding, he almost didn't attend because he felt awkward going stag. He was performing his patented wallflower act when he saw her walking toward the bar. It was the kind of woman his Granddaddy used to refer to as a "burlap bag full of bobcat," until he met Jennifer he never really understood what that meant. She wore the proverbial little black dress which fit her perfectly. Curves in all the right places and exquisitely proportioned, she walked with an easy grace yet oozed raw sexuality. Dirty-blond hair fell to her shoulders and her face was, to him, stunning. He quickly strode to the bar arriving a moment before she did so she had to stand behind him in line.

He turned to her before ordering. "Buy you a drink?

"Drinks are free."

"What can I say? I'm a big spender."

She rolled her eyes as she smiled at him. "Vodka and tonic with a twist."

"Exactly what I was having except mine is beer."

She laughed. "So it's the same, but different."

"Exactly!"

He took the drinks from the bartender and handed her the vodka as they stepped away from the line. His heart started racing as she made no move to walk away from him.

"I'm Luke." He held out his hand.

"Jennifer."

Before he could figure out which corny pickup line to use a sharp-looking guy in an expensively tailored suit walked over. He was a head taller and thirty pounds of pure muscle heavier, in short, the perfect match for the smoking hot babe in the little black dress. Luke could feel himself deflate as his ego took a blow. How could he have thought a girl like her would be interested in him?

"There you are," the tall, handsome dude said.

She turned to go. "It was nice meeting you."

Luke reclaimed his spot against the wall hanging with the other single guys and men who wanted to get away from their wives and girlfriends. While they chatted about football and other he-manly things he kept his eye out for Jennifer. He caught glimpses of her laughing it up with a group of people having totally forgotten, he was sure, that he existed. He made his exit as soon as it was polite to do so.

Fate intervened a few weeks later at a party thrown by the newly-married couple. It was a very casual affair at their new apartment. They had recently returned from their honeymoon and wanted to continue the party by inviting several friends over. Luke had no qualms about being alone this time because it didn't require a suit, jeans and a t-shirt were fine. Soon after he arrived he went into the kitchen and grabbed a Sam Adams out of the fridge.

"Lucas, right?" said a voice behind him

"Only when I'm in serious trouble, otherwise it's Luke."

He turned around and his heart skipped a beat, he hadn't recognized the voice. She wore form-hugging jeans with a white, button-down shirt, hair tied back, and a face even more beautiful that he remembered. He didn't see anyone with her but he assumed her guy was in the other room.

"I suppose you want me to buy you another drink."

"Nah, I'll just take that." She grabbed the beer right out of his hand.

He got another one out of the fridge and they clinked bottles.

"Sorry we didn't have much chance to chat," Jennifer said.

"Your boyfriend might have gotten upset. Then I'd have to beat him up and, well, that would have been ugly."

She smiled. "He wasn't my boyfriend, he was my cousin. I didn't want to go alone; you know how guys can be when they see a solo female at a wedding."

"I wouldn't know, I never see solo females at weddings."

"That's because we all drag our cousins along."

"So it's like a system. Do they teach you that in 'hot chick' school?"

"More like the school of bad dates. So Luke, what do you do when you're not buying women free drinks?"

"I'm in advertising."

"Like *Mad Men*?"

"Exactly like *Mad Men*, only totally opposite."

She laughed. "Sounds exciting."

"It is exciting, except that it's excruciatingly boring."

Luke remembered nothing about the party but Jennifer. They had a blast but when it was time to go he started feeling uneasy. He knew he had to ask her for her number but he was, as usual, fearing rejection. It was the same problem he had selling advertising. He would do a fantastic presentation, the client would be giving off buying signals galore but he still couldn't close the deal. His manager told him he would always have trouble meeting quota if he didn't learn to ask for the order. Jennifer slipped away from him once, he wasn't going to let it happen again – not without a fight anyway. He asked for the order.

They dated for several months and it just kept getting better. His friends would ask how he ever got someone like her and he answered honestly – he didn't have a clue. They went out one Friday night but Jennifer wasn't her bubbly self. He waited for her to tell him what was wrong but she never did so he eventually asked her. She said that she had to move out of the apartment that she loved. The house had been sold and the new owner wanted the space for his mother. Luke casually said that she could move into his place until she found something. He was ecstatic when she not only agreed but was enthusiastic about it. She never found a place, or tried to.

Luke grew to love Jennifer more than he ever thought possible. He couldn't imagine, nor did he want to, ever being with anyone else. He scraped together every dime he had and maxed out his credit cards to borrow a few thousand more so he could buy her a magnificent diamond. He took her to her favorite restaurant and tried to act calm but was a nervous wreck. With the wait staff, kitchen help, and every customer in the place watching he moved next to Jennifer and dropped to one knee.

Luke held out the box with the ring. "Jennifer, I love you more than life itself. Will you marry me? Will you be my wife?"

Jennifer's eyes went wide, her mouth hung open in shock as the tears started rolling down her face. Unable to find words, she nodded vigorously as he slipped the ring on her finger. The restaurant erupted with applause as she threw her arms around him. His only regret was that his Granddaddy would never meet the love of his life.

Now the wedding was almost here. The photographer and the hall had been given deposits but the balance was due. Combined the total was just under three thousand dollars. Luke checked his bank balance – two hundred forty-seven dollars and sixteen cents. He was days away from receiving his semi-annual bonus and that should cover it with a few dollars to spare. Worst case, he may have to stall paying the caterers for a day or two.

Luke went to the office a little later that morning. There was a nervous energy in the air. Those who had hit their sales targets were in animated moods as they tried to calculate what their bonus might be. Other salespeople who missed quota were hoping that they were close enough to retain their jobs. Still others knew there was no hope and were quietly packing their things. He hated this time. Whenever he looked at the Lucite award on his desk that declared he was MVP of Sales he felt like a fraud. It was for his first campaign three years earlier. A new account with a huge budget had fallen into his lap vaulting him well beyond quota resulting in a bonus that nearly doubled his salary. The next campaign he fell so far below quota that he would have been fired had he not been the MVP previously. Last time he was below target again but only by a couple of percentage points. No bonus, but he still had a job.

This time all his major clients renewed. He lost several smaller accounts but brought in just enough new business to hit a little beyond his quota and qualify for a bonus. It wouldn't be a big one but it would cover the wedding. Throughout the day people were being having a conference with their managers to go over their numbers and learn their fate. For once he wasn't dreading the meeting.

He was called in a little after three that afternoon. Walter, his manager, looked haggard from what had to be his most stressful day of the year. He saw his file on the desk as he sat in the chair across from Walter.

"Have you seen this?" Walter asked as he tossed the business section of that day's Review Journal on the desk.

He grabbed the paper and scanned it. Blood rushed from his head and he felt faint. His biggest account had filed for bankruptcy and was closing their doors. He never had clue they were in trouble.

"Accounting has already reversed the sale. Had they waited three more days to file it would have counted against the next campaign and you would have had time to make it up."

"But I need that money."

"Luke, I'm sorry. This puts you so far below quota that you should be terminated but I've convinced them to hold off for now."

"For now?"

"You're being placed on performance review instead. You'll be reevaluated after sixty days. You have to make up the loss and be on target for quota for the new campaign by then."

"But that's impossible. You can't do that in sixty days."

"I did the best I could; I know you have the wedding coming up. Luke, it's time to look for something else, you're too nice a guy for this business."

Luke was in shock. He walked out of Walter's office, past his own desk and out the door. He had no recollection of driving home or retrieving his Granddaddy's gun from the mantel. The Colt was originally owned by his great-great-grandfather and handed down through the years. Luke's father died when he was just a baby but his Granddaddy had always been there. The Colt was more than a gun. It was skinned knees, little league games, parent-teacher conferences, being caught smoking behind the garage, every hug, every punishment, every laugh, every tear – it *was* his Granddaddy. Granddaddy was dead now, so it goes.

Luke parked in front of the storefront in the seedier part of downtown Las Vegas. The gun and box of cartridges sat on the seat beside him. He waited there for a long time working up the nerve to go in. He watched someone come out and the place now appeared to be empty. He took a deep breath and got out of the car. His hands were shaking as he pushed the door open and went inside. The only person he could see was a middle-aged man working behind the counter, there were no customers. The clerk turned and walked in his direction.

"Can I help you?"

Luke held up the gun. "I want three thousand dollars."

Luke was sitting on the sofa when Jennifer came home. She looked puzzled when she saw the stacks of bills on the coffee table. She tossed her purse down and glanced at the empty space on mantel and back at him.

"Luke, what's going on? Where's your grandfather's pistol?"

He looked up at her as the tears started to flow. She sat next to him and hugged him close to her until he was able to speak. When he calmed down he told her everything; she refused to let go. When he was finished she kissed him softly before pulling away a little.

"Luke, honey, I love you so much, but you are a stupid, stupid man."

"I love you, that's why I did it."

She stood up and held out her hand. "Come on, let's go."

"Go where?"

"To the pawnshop to get back Granddaddy's gun."

Meet the Authors

Nancy Buford

Nancy Buford, writing as Noëlle de Beaufort, weaves insights from her background in finance with her studies of French language, culture and literature and her love of history, travel, art and cultures into the historical romantic suspense and adventure genre. She is working on several novels delving into multiple generations of a family from its origins in France through its migration to England and beyond.

She holds a B.A. summa cum laude in French Literature from Denison University and an M.B.A. in Finance and International Business from New York University. After many years in New York City and Los Angeles, she now lives in Las Vegas with two fascinating felines.

Karen Bryant

Karen Bryant is a Las Vegas writer and would-be chocolatier who has recently combined these two passions in a cross-country drive visiting and blogging about the US chocolate experience (www.redwhiteandchocolate.com). She has previously published magazine articles and a monthly column about mid-life women who reinvented themselves. She is also venturing into fiction, which is making family and friends nervous - all that good material! In addition to writing, she is the Executive Director of the Fine Chocolate Industry Association. She has two grown children in California who look forward to her short stories and bonbons.

Jay Hill

Jay Hill writes crime fiction and meta-modern narratives incorporating experiences and insights from practicing law and living in Italy and Las Vegas. He has completed and is editing two crime fiction "why-done-it" novels set in Las Vegas and is working on a metamodern philosophical novella set in 1970's Italy exploring the metaxy between an awareness of the transience of things and moral responsibility. He also writes short stories and poetry.

He attended Ohio University and has a B.S. and a J.D. from The University of Cincinnati where he studied creative writing under David Schloss. He and his wife, Janet, lived in Italy before settling in Las Vegas.

Jay can be reached at jayhillauthor@gmail.com

John Hill

John Hill was a full-time professional Hollywood TV and screenwriter from 1974- 1999. His credits include *Griffin and Phoenix* (1976), *Heartbeeps* (1981), co-writer of *Little Nikita* (1988) and *Quigley Down Under*, (1990). He has worked on staff as a writer-type producer on *Quantum Leap* and on *L.A. Law*, where he won an Emmy in 1991. He now teaches writing and filmmaking at the University of Nevada in Las Vegas, where he lives with his wife Nancy.

John was the winner of the 2013 *Jay MacLarty Founders Award* from the Las Vegas Writers Group.

Hyrum Husky, Jr.

Hyrum Huskey, Jr. is a Las Vegas retiree. After three separate "careers" as a commissioned Army Officer, college Dean of Student Services, and a public transit manager, he hopes to continue his lifetime of underpaid writing fun. He previously published one nonfiction book (Herald House, 1980) and wrote news and feature articles for four years at *The Montague Reporter*, a New England weekly newspaper in MA. Hyrum has also published articles and humor poetry in *Messing About in Boats*, *Scuttlebutt*, and in various education journals. He is an avid reader of writing books, and a frequent conference attendee, when he actually should have his butt in a chair, writing.

Patricia Kranish

I love living in the past and set much of my fiction in the Ice Age — even though I hate being cold and left New York seven years ago to live in Las Vegas. While tramping around Nevada's breathtaking mountains with like-minded, but more agile, nature enthusiasts, I started investigating the oldest mummy ever found — and that includes King Tut who is 6,000 years younger. Imagine the life of people who lived when glaciers from the north were still spitting up mountains and Nevada was beneath a deep blue sea. *Lake Lahontan*, takes us further back to draw a picture of the time the fickle and demanding Ice Age climate carried a false hope of spring and the people were willing to sacrifice anything to preserve its warmth.

Holly Mack

Holly Mack enjoys writing and reading about the supernatural. At the age of thirteen she made her first trip to a psychic, and got hooked on the drama and storytelling of the new-age prophets. Continuing her visits, she began to notice certain whispered conversations taking place among the professionals. It opened her eyes to the common pettiness inherent in any job, nine-to-five or not. This story is a love letter to the hard-working, regular people who keep mystery and excitement alive.

Carole McKinnis

My husband and I have lived in Las Vegas a long, long time.

We were singers in so many large voice and orchestra productions, operas and oratorios.

In those singing years I was a soloist in classical productions of "The Messiah", "The Brahms Christmas Mass" and the Vivaldi, "Gloria".

This was a great time for seeing the various world views of singers and musicians.

It was fun sorting through those memories for the characters in "Who Sits at The Left Hand of God."

Ernest Walwyn

Ernest Walwyn started writing poetry and short stories while attending school in the Bronx, New York. He spent 26 years in the Air Force during which time the only writing done was for college courses. He has BAs in Resource Management and Information Systems Management. He has poems published in "Who's Who in American Poetry" for 2013 and 2014 and "Centres for Expression" by Noble House. "Her Mother's Daughter is a short story included in "Slaughter House: The Serial Killer". Two other short stories pending publication are "Wolf" by Chaosium and "Malcolm's House" by James Ward Kirk. He lives in North Las Vegas with his wife Monika.

Richard J. Warren

Richard Warren is an author, freelance journalist and teaches English Composition at the University of Nevada, Las Vegas. He is currently the Consumer Columnist for *The Vegas Voice* newspaper. Richard is also the author of *A Rehabber's Tale: The Reality of Fixing and Flipping Real Estate* and has written more than 150 articles related to real estate investing. His latest book, *Scammers, Schemers, and Dreamers*, was released in June 2014. Co-written with Elisabeth Daniels, the former head of the *Nevada Fight Fraud Task Force*, the book explores the human toll of being victimized by fraud.

Additionally Richard is a past president of the Writers of Southern Nevada and currently serves on its board of directors.

The Las Vegas Writers Group

A Brief History

Founded by Jay MacLarty and Vic Cravello, the Las Vegas Writers Group has grown from its humble beginnings to become the premier writers group in Southern Nevada. Jay had travelled a long, hard road to publication which included 50 rejections before finally landing an agent and signing a deal with Simon & Shuster. The LVWG was a way for him to help others achieve what he had. His vision was a group that was a mix of successfully published and aspiring authors. It has grown far beyond what anyone expected.

The group, originally known as The Literati, held its first official meeting in September 2004 with four writers attending. Monthly gatherings took place in a coffee shop and the group grew slowly through word of mouth. By January of 2007 the membership had increased to the point that the meetings moved to a local pub. Establishing an internet presence through Meetup accelerated the growth rate and the group sought out a larger venue to accommodate the increasing attendance. Today membership stands at more than 400 writers with monthly meetings typically attended by 70 or more published and aspiring authors.

There are a number of reasons for the success of the group. First there is no profit motive, the meeting fee is kept as low as possible and is used to cover the cost of running the group and putting on the meetings with any excess going toward the annual holiday party and producing this anthology. Second is the quality of the monthly program. Speakers are generally individuals with something valuable to share with the members regarding both the craft and business of writing. Past presenters have included Creative Writing Faculty from UNLV, authors from major publishing houses, Emmy Award winning screenwriters, Pulitzer Prize nominees, and most recently an O' Henry Award winning writer. Lastly, and most importantly, the LVWG thrives due to the dedication of the volunteers who through there tireless efforts have helped make the group what it is today.

Made in the USA
Charleston, SC
09 January 2016